The Iron Dragon

The Courageous Story of Lee Chin

Bonnie Pryor

Enslow Publishers, Inc.
40 Industrial Road
Box 398
Berkeley Heights, NJ 07922
USA

http://www.enslow.com

Tonya, with love

This book is a work of fiction. References to real people, events, establishments, organizations, or locales are intended only to provide a sense of authenticity, and are used to advance the fictional narrative. All other characters, and all incidents and dialogue, are drawn from the author's imagination and are not to be construed as real.

Library of Congress Cataloging-in-Publication Data:

Pryor, Bonnie.
    The iron dragon : the courageous story of Lee Chin / Bonnie Pryor.
       p. cm. — (Historical fiction adventures (HFA))
    Summary: Teenager Lee Chin leaves China and goes to California to work on the transcontinental railroad, where he defies his father's wishes, saves his money to free his younger sister from slavery in China, and brings her to join him in order to begin a new life in America. Includes historical note about the Chinese who helped build the transcontinental railroad.
    Includes bibliographical references (p.   )
    ISBN 978-0-7660-3389-4 (Library Ed.)
    ISBN 978-1-59845-215-0 (Paperback Ed.)
    1. Chinese—United States—Juvenile fiction. 2. Chinese Americans—Juvenile fiction. [1. Chinese—United States—Fiction. 2. Chinese Americans—Fiction. 3. Emigration and immigration—Fiction. 4. Railroads—Fiction. 5. California—History—1850-1950—Fiction.] I. Title.
    PZ7.P94965Ir 2010
    [Fic]—dc22   2009017930

Printed in the United States of America

062010 Lake Book Manufacturing, Inc., Melrose Park, IL

10 9 8 7 6 5 4 3 2 1

To Our Readers: We have done our best to make sure all Internet Addresses in this book were active and appropriate when we went to press. However, the author and the publisher have no control over and assume no liability for the material available on those Internet sites or on other Web sites they may link to. Any comments or suggestions can be sent by e-mail to comments@enslow.com or to the address on the back cover.

♻ Enslow Publishers, Inc., is committed to printing our books on recycled paper. The paper in every book contains 10% to 30% post-consumer waste (PCW). The cover board on the outside of each book contains 100% PCW. Our goal is to do our part to help young people and the environment too!

Illustration Credits: Enslow Publishers, Inc., p. 152; *Harper's Weekly* / Library of Congress, p. 155; Library of Congress, pp. 153, 157; Original Painting by © Corey Wolfe, p. 1.

Cover Illustration: Original Painting by © Corey Wolfe.

 Contents

chapter one

Storm at Sea

Late Spring 1866

The storm had started hours ago with black clouds rolling across the sky and lightning jagging down to the sea. A merciless wind whipped the white-capped waves that battered the ship and washed over the highest deck. We had been ordered belowdecks, uncomfortable, frightened, and grumbling, squeezed into the tiny space where we slept. I was curled in my narrow bunk fighting desperately as usual to keep down my supper. In all my twelve years I could not remember feeling so miserable. This was worse than the months of famine, when some days all we had was hot water flavored with reused tea leaves and a few mouthfuls of rice.

From the narrow gangway, I could hear the shriek of wind as the ship was tossed from side to side. On the deck above, the sailors' shouts and curses were sucked away by

the wind. The words were foreign, but I recognized the fear in their voices as they battled the storm.

Across the crowd I saw my father watching me. I understood the shame he felt for his youngest son. While many had been seasick at the start of the voyage a few weeks ago, most had recovered in a few days after leaving Guangzhou, which was also called Canton. I, however, had been sick nearly the whole journey, forced by my weak stomach to curl up in my bed, clutching my slop bucket.

A rush of water suddenly poured down the hatch, drenching the men. But from above I heard the hatchway closing and the bolt to hold it slide into place. It was too dangerous to burn the lanterns when the ship was being battered by the waves. Someone, I thought it might have been my father, gave the order to extinguish the few lanterns. The room was plunged into darkness.

I fought my rising panic. What if the ship sank? We were locked belowdecks with no chance to escape. Even though I knew there would be no chance to survive in the stormy ocean, dying trapped belowdecks seemed so much more terrifying. If we died at sea, our bones could not be buried in the Celestial Kingdom, the name we call our country of China. I might not find my way to the other side, a place ruled by the Jade Emperor. This is like the white man's heaven. I bit my lip to keep from crying out.

The ship was so overcrowded that there was barely enough space to walk between the narrow bunks. Every day, I had listened to men's petty squabbles and their complaining until I wanted to scream out for them to be quiet. Of course, I would never be so disrespectful to my elders. Although, sometimes I liked to think about what their shocked faces would look like if I was. Now, however, although the room was just as crowded, there was an uncanny silence as each man seemed to contemplate his fate.

Between the violent motion of the ship, someone squeezed into the small space at the end of the bunk.

"Lee Chin, are you still sick?" my elder cousin Yi asked in his soft voice. It was too dark to see Yi's usually cheerful face, but I knew it would be scrunched with sympathy.

I nodded, and then realized my cousin could not see it. "If I don't see land soon, I believe I will die," I moaned.

"It is lucky for you we did not sign up to be fishermen," Yi said.

I laughed in spite of my misery. Yi could always cheer me up. "When we get to Gold Mountain I will never step on a boat again," I declared.

"Then how will you get home with all your riches?" Yi teased. "I am going to save my money, and when I go home I will buy much land. Then I will take a wife, or maybe two wives, and a servant girl to bring me hot tea and comb

my hair." Yi's voice faltered. "I am sorry, Little Cousin. I was told that your father sold your little sister when the famine started."

I was glad that my cousin could not see the tears welling in my eyes. I thought of little Sunshine. I could still hear her giggle when I teased her. She liked to follow me around, and even if I chased her away, she would hide nearby, peeking at me with her sparkling eyes.

"She was only a worthless girl," I said gruffly, hiding my sadness. "Perhaps my father will buy her back when we return."

Yi was silent. I felt the ship rise suddenly and then come down with a mighty crack. I reached for the wooden post, but my body was wrenched violently forward, and for a brief, terrifying second, I had the sensation of flying. Then I landed with a painful thump wedged against the next bunk. Yi flew after me, landing on top. I heard a thump as Yi's head hit the post. At the same instant, his knee smashed into my stomach with such force that I gasped, unable to catch my breath. The slop bucket rattled across the floor, spilling the contents, and the stench made it even harder to breathe. Around the room I could hear groans and fearful moaning. Some of the men cursed; others prayed to the gods for protection.

After a moment I caught my breath. I pushed at Yi's motionless body. "Cousin Yi," I gasped. "Are you all right?"

"Except for a broken head," Yi answered in a muffled voice, after an anxious moment. He untangled himself from me and we climbed back on the bunk as another wave slammed the boat. This time both of us managed to hold on.

The bedlam continued as the ship wildly pitched with wave after wave. Water poured in through the cracks from the deck overhead, soaking the straw-filled mattresses, the blankets, and our clothes. It was the longest night I had ever lived through—even counting the nights I had lain awake, hunger gnawing at my stomach.

The famine had come after the drought one year and floods the next had destroyed the crops. On those nights, I had taken a paper and drawing pencil and sketched out the farm in happier days. My hunger was forgotten as I sketched the small chicken house, and Mo the ox, who had patiently pulled the plow before my father had been forced to kill him for food.

Sometimes I sketched Sunshine, who, like her name, was always smiling even as her body grew gaunt with starvation. I thought about the last time that I had seen her. She was sitting outside our door while my father informed my mother that he had sold Sunshine to the richest man in our district to be a servant. "She would have died soon," he said, when my mother cried. "She will help in the kitchen and have food to eat. She will be better off than the rest of

us," he added harshly, when my mother continued to wail. "We will take the money and go to the city to find work."

The storm raged on through most of the night, but by morning, the waves had lessened and I was so exhausted that I managed a short, fitful sleep. I awoke to the sound of the hatchway cover being opened. Bright sunlight filtered into the room. The older men muttered angrily among themselves, and they chose a spokesman to make an official protest.

"It won't do any good," Yi said sleepily. "It will be just like when they complained about the food."

The light was strong enough now for me to notice dried blood on Yi's face. A large lump was over his right eye. "You are hurt, Elder Cousin."

"No more than you Little Cousin," Yi said, gingerly touching his head.

I examined my own body. Although every inch of me hurt, I seemed all right, except for bruises. Then I touched my eye and winced.

"It has turned purple," Yi said, chuckling. "It looks like you have been fighting a dragon."

"I think it was more like your elbow," I replied with a smile.

Yi went off to find Zhang Wei, who had knowledge of healing herbs. My clean shirt was wet from the storm, but I put it on anyway. Then I took my filthy shirt and carried the bucket up to the main deck to fetch water to wash it. The day had dawned with blue skies and a placid sea. I realized that for the first time I was not seasick. My belly rumbled with hunger. I took my bowl of oatmeal and ate it all, although many of the men grumbled that there was no rice.

Later that morning I sat on the main deck with the small group learning English from Wu Chang. An agent from the Six Companies had given each of us a paper with simple phrases in English to learn. For most of the men, my father included, that was all they needed.

The Six Companies was made up of rich merchants, and each company represented an area back home. They would tend to all our needs. It was an agent of the Six Companies who had hired us to build the railroad and advanced us the money for the passage. The agent would take the seventy-five dollars fare from the first few months' wages. The agent would also handle shipments of food to the camps—rice, dried mushrooms, fish, and vegetables—and they would send money back home and handle shipping a body back home for burial should the worst happen. For most of the men, that was enough. They were here to work and send money back home, and wanted little to do with the hairy, smelly barbarians. If the men had a problem, the Six Companies would help them, not the white man.

I was curious about the Americans. That they did not bathe often enough was true, but I wanted to learn their language so I could learn more about them. Wu Chang, who had been a gold miner for two years and spoke the language, told my father that he had never seen anyone learn as fast as me.

My father had not looked particularly pleased at this praise. My father obviously thought it was another useless skill like my drawing. But he allowed me to attend the classes.

Yi sat down beside me. The herb doctor had applied a poultice of herbs and a healing salve, and wrapped Yi's head with a strip of cloth.

A peal of laughter from the upper deck made us look up. A tall American man stood talking with a woman. The woman wore a dress of green silk with billowing skirts. Her hair was the color of straw and was wound into curls. She slipped her arm around the man's arm and laughed again.

"The American women are very bold," I said. I thought of my mother, who wore simple cotton trousers and a shirt. She always walked modestly, a few steps behind my father.

"Americans are barbarians," Yi said cheerfully. "But they will pay us well. In a few years, we can return to China as rich men."

Today, Wu Chang was teaching us the different parts of the body. My thoughts drifted away. I itched to draw all the

new sites I had been seeing. I did not have the paints to capture the brightly colored dress of the barbarians, or the freshly washed blue of the sky. But my pencil could have sketched the ship. Now that my stomach was still, I could admire the three tall masts and the large paddlewheel on the side that kept us moving even when there was no wind.

I could hear the steady drone of the engines keeping the wheel turning. Wu Chang had told us that when he made his first trip to America, it had taken several months on a sailing ship. Now it took less than three weeks.

Yi poked me gently on my side. "You are daydreaming, Little Cousin. How will you know how to say 'elbow,' if one should land on your other eye?"

chapter two

An Unfriendly Welcome

The agent of the Six Companies was waiting when we finally arrived at the San Francisco, California, dock. I was astonished at the bustling city with its prosperous shops dotting the hilly streets. The clamorous sounds of iron and machinery being unloaded by burly men onto wagons and carts made me wish I could wander around and observe. But our group was gathered together at one end of a wooden dock. The representative appeared rich, both in his manner and his dress. He was plump and seemed annoyed, as though there were any number of places he would rather be. He was impeccably groomed and his hair was smoothly oiled and braided. He flicked at an imaginary speck of dust on his embroidered green silk jacket while he waited for us to assemble with our boxes and bags. A clerk, considerably less grand, sat at a small table checking names in a large ledger and changing Chinese *cash,* the name of our coins, for American money.

I fingered the rawhide thong around my neck. I had earned a little money running some errands before the ship had sailed. The *cash* had a hole in the middle, making it easy to string.

"I am going to change my money," I told Yi. "Maybe there will be somewhere nearby to purchase drawing paper."

"Your father will not be happy if he sees you," Yi said sympathetically.

I flushed guiltily. "I want to draw all this before I forget," I said, waving my arm at the teeming dock. "I will only draw after work."

When I stepped up to the agent, he frowned. "This boy is too young," he declared, tapping the very long nail on his little finger against his ample stomach. "Mr. Crocker will not allow one so young to work on the railroad."

My father bowed low. "My son is worthless, but he is a hard worker. I had to leave the eldest sons at home to care for my land."

I did not take offense at my father's words. It is not polite to brag about one's children, nor is it wise to draw the attention of the gods. In my case, though, I suspected my father really did think of me as worthless because I was not interested in working the land or being a farmer. For a minute I was pleased that he had called me a hard worker, until I realized that he merely wanted to make certain I got a job so I could send money home.

Some of the men were assigned special jobs. Zhang Wei, the herb doctor, had been chosen to be a cook. "Our group is larger than most. There are nearly forty men. I could use some help. The boy is learning to speak the white man's language. That may be useful."

My father looked at me. "Then he will not be living in my camp."

"I will watch over him," Yi said quickly. "I too am in this group."

"Then it is done. The men will have to pay a little more to cover your wages. You can see your son on Sundays, when you have a day off," the agent said firmly, as he made a mark in his ledger book.

My father was not an affectionate man, and I was not his favorite son. He looked at me briefly. "Make your ancestors proud," was all he said.

"I will, Honorable Father," I answered. There was an ache in my heart, but there was no time to dwell on it. The agent divided us into our assigned groups and led us to another busy dock. There, we were informed we would have to board another steamer for the trip to Sacramento. From there, the agent explained, we would ride the train, which the men called the Iron Dragon, to the work site.

I groaned, but Yi chuckled and gave my shoulder a friendly cuff. "It is only a short trip, Little Cousin. Tomorrow we will be on land again. And look," he said,

pointing to a cart that had just arrived with several large pots. "They are going to feed us."

Each man was given a bowl of rice with vegetables and small pieces of pork. We gobbled the food eagerly, happy to be eating familiar food. As we ate, I noticed a small crowd of rough, scowling men gathering around us. They made no attempt to hide their hostility as they pointed at us and shouted angry words. Off to one side, I saw a strange thing. A man set up a small three-legged table with a box on it. Over that he draped a cloth. Then he ducked underneath the cloth.

"Do you see that?" I asked Yi.

Yi laughed. "I saw that in Guangzhou. It is some kind of new invention that makes pictures."

I was confused. "How can he paint under there with no good light?" I asked.

The smile slid from Yi's face as he glanced at the still-growing crowd. The men shouted and jeered at us, and although I did not understand the words, I knew that they were shouting insults.

The men in our group stood stoically, even when the ruffians picked up stones and threw them. A small stone hit me on the back of my neck. I turned, unable to hold my anger, but suddenly Zhang Wei was there behind me.

"Look over there," he said, as though nothing was happening. "They have lowered the gangplank for us to board the ship."

"Why are those men shouting at us?" I asked, rubbing my neck.

"They say we are taking jobs away from them, but the agent said they hired us because they couldn't find enough good workers," Zhang Wei answered. He steered us to the gangplank like a mother hen with her chicks. "They say we are heathens because we do not know their god."

I was silent as we boarded the steamer. My excitement at all the new sights had turned to uneasiness. I leaned on the railing, watching the tide of angry faces. What kind of country was this, where they hated you for the gods you honored? I felt a moment of shame. Hadn't I called the Americans barbarians? But that was because they were loud and did not bathe often enough to keep from smelling. I had not called them barbarians for what they thought.

The steamship was even more crowded than the ship we had taken from China. This time, however, we were not required to go belowdecks. It was a fine, clear night and we squeezed together on the main deck. Just as before, the white people had comfortable sleeping cabins while we were confined to the deck. Yi secured us a small spot and had already rolled out our sleeping mats. At least the sky was clear, with no signs of a storm. I closed my eyes,

intending to nap, but when the ship's loud horn woke me, I discovered that the whole night had passed and we were about to dock in Sacramento.

Yi had already rolled away his mat. "You must have been tired, Little Cousin. I was about to wonder if you had gone to the other side."

A cup of tea and a small bowl of rice awaited each man as we crowded together on the dock. I watched nervously as I ate. Although the white men's faces were not friendly, at least there were no threatening crowds.

As soon as we were finished, we were given directions to the railroad. I walked slowly, falling behind the group as I peered into many of the shop windows. Finally, Yi said in exasperation, "Little Cousin. We are going to get lost."

"You go on and keep my place," I said. "This store looks like the kind to have paper. I will catch up."

"I promised your father I would care for you," Yi protested.

"I will catch up. You go on," I insisted. I took out the small square of cloth holding the money I had exchanged at the dock. I ducked into the store, ignoring Yi's unhappy face.

There were several people in the store. A tall man with a drooping mustache was sorting through a stack of shirts. A man wearing a white apron, who I decided must be the clerk, was talking with a lady examining bolts of material.

I waited politely, but the clerk looked up and said roughly, "We don't sell to you Chinks."

Not understanding his words, I bowed and repeated the words I had learned from Wu Chang. "Please, sir. I would like to buy paper."

"I told you we don't sell to no heathens," the man shouted. "Now get out."

I froze. I could not understand what the man was saying, but obviously he was angry. Had I not said the words correctly? Maybe I had said something offensive. I quickly untied my cloth. "I have money," I said.

The man swept his hand out, knocking the money out of my hand and sending it rolling across the floor. I looked at my meager savings disappearing under counters and cabinets. I scrambled to retrieve my coins, but the man grabbed a broom that was leaning against the wall and raised it over his head as if to strike me.

I had not even seen the man with the mustache move, but suddenly he was there, grabbing the clerk's hand and twisting it until the broom dropped with a clatter on the floor. "I don't think that's necessary," he said calmly. "The boy just asked to buy paper."

"We don't sell to heathen Chinese," the man repeated stubbornly.

"Then you can sell it to me," said the big man. Meanwhile, I scooped up the few coins I could see and

scurried toward the door. But before I left, the mustached man grabbed my arm.

"What kind of paper do you want?" he asked.

I shook my head to show I didn't understand, but the man gave me a shrewd look. "Anybody that desperate for paper must be an artist." He made motions like he was drawing.

I nodded and he considered several types of paper neatly arranged on a shelf. He finally selected a large, nicely bound book with creamy white paper and handed it to me.

I bowed low, grinning with delight. Hugging the paper to my chest, I held out my coins to the man, wondering if it was enough. The man shook his head, reaching into his pockets, but I thrust my hand forward again. I did not want the man to think I was a beggar. The man looked at me and, as though he understood, looked at the coins in my hand and picked up two of them.

"Wait," the lady cried out. Going to the shelf, she carefully considered. Then she picked up four color sticks—red, yellow, green, and blue—and handed them to me. Like the man, she carefully selected several coins from my hands. I again bowed my thanks. At home, I had only had a charcoal pencil, although I had tried to make colors by crushing berries, leaves, and even rocks. Now I could make real paintings. Even though the Americans were

barbarians, they were capable of great kindness. I was not so sure anyone would have helped me if I had been in the Celestial Kingdom. I pointed to myself. "Lee Chin," I said.

The man stuck out his hand. "Clay McGee," he said.

Startled, I jumped back. Then I remembered that Wu Chang had told us that this was how the Americans greeted each other, unlike in China, where it meant you wanted to fight. Clay McGee vigorously pumped the hand I cautiously held out.

When McGee let loose of my hand, I realized how long I had been in the store. Bowing again, I ran out the door. I had a moment of panic when I didn't see any of my countrymen. Then not too far off I heard several long, low blasts of a horn. Hoping that I was hearing the sound of the train, I raced off.

chapter three

The Railroad

As I rounded the corner, I heaved a sigh of relief. There was my group, and there was Yi, anxiously pacing at the edge of the crowd. He waved at me, and I ran over to meet him.

"I was worried," he said crossly.

"I am sorry to worry you, Elder Cousin," I said. "But look what I bought."

He admired the tablet and drawing sticks before I tucked them carefully into my pack next to the picture of my mother and Sunshine. I had made that picture in happier times. I covered them with my change of clothes and my rolled-up sleeping mat.

The air was filled with cinders and smoke. "Is there a fire?" I exclaimed. I looked around me. Everywhere I looked there were stacks of lumber, long iron rails, and boxes of other supplies. Scores of men scurried around, loading them onto flat wagons. The wagons' wheels were perched on a road of the very same iron rails that I saw in

the stacks. I could see they were also fastened to a huge machine, belching smoke and cinders from a giant chimney. "Is that the Iron Dragon?" I gasped.

"It belches smoke like a dragon," Yi said. "The Americans call it a lo-co-mo-tive."

Right behind the locomotive was an enclosed wagon. I could see a crowd of white people gathering around it.

Yi pointed. "See those iron tracks? That's what we are going to build. I heard some men talking. They are going to build the tracks across the country. They are going to make tunnels through the mountains."

I pulled my new tablet out of my bag and quickly sketched the locomotive. When I looked up from my drawing, I noticed my father watching me through the crowd. His face was pinched with disapproval.

Yi's face, however, was beaming. "That is such a wonderful picture. I think you will be a famous artist someday."

I bent back to my work, drawing the plain square building that I guessed was where the passengers paid their fare. There were several women there with wide skirts and hair the color of straw.

Suddenly, there was a heavy hand on my shoulder. Alarmed, I looked up to see the face of the man in the store, Clay McGee. He pointed to the tablet, and I thought he wanted to take it from me. Then I realized he was asking to see my drawing. Wordlessly, I handed it to him.

Zhang Wei and Yi crowded close, along with several other men. I realized they were trying to protect me. Even my father looked alarmed and had started to push his way through the crowd.

"I know this man," I said in my language. "He is a friend."

Clay McGee did not seem to notice the commotion he had caused. He pounded my back again. "That is a right good drawing," he exclaimed heartily. "I knew you were an artist."

Although his words were foreign, I did understand his friendly face. Impulsively, I tore the drawing from the tablet and handed it to him.

"Thank you," he said, and he bowed. Then, finally noticing the unfriendly-looking crowd of my countrymen, he waved and hurried away. I saw him showing the drawing to several white people by the ticket office.

"You should be careful not to draw attention to your-self," my father said disapprovingly. "The white people are not our friends. They are not to be trusted. How do you know such a man?"

The call to board the train saved me from having to answer questions. "Stay with your own people," my father said sharply. Then he turned away abruptly and hurried off to rejoin his group.

I stared after him unhappily. My father was proud of his two eldest sons, who were sturdy and strong, and talked mostly of seeds, plows, and crops. I was small and slim like my mother, and nothing I did ever pleased him. Although he sometimes begrudgingly gave me a coin to buy paper when we went to our small village to sell our extra rice, he said that drawing was womanly. That puzzled me because all the great painters in China are men. But that was the way he thought.

With a sigh, I watched as the Americans, including my new friend McGee, boarded the passenger car. Instead of boarding the passenger cars, we were herded to the cars that were loaded with freight. I followed Yi to a flat car piled high with lumber, wooden boxes, and barrels. We clambered over the boxes and finally found a small space to squeeze into. I was growing more apprehensive by the minute. I envied McGee, safe inside the passenger car. Yi had seen inside and said they had padded seats. Our seat was a rough board.

The locomotive gave several loud blasts of the horn. The Iron Dragon lurched forward. Yi's face turned pale, and his knuckles were white from gripping the edge of the board that was our seat. Thick black smoke drifted back, making us cough and choke. In spite of this, after a few minutes, I was enjoying the ride immensely.

The Railroad

Suddenly, Yi groaned. We were approaching a high wooden trestle. It seemed much too flimsy to hold such a tremendous weight, but the Iron Dragon continued across it without difficulty. Far below us, I could see a river.

The train made a steady clickity-clack kind of noise, flying across the rails. I settled back and decided I liked this locomotive travel. It was exciting to have a part in building a railroad, even if it was only to help feed the men who did the work.

The train paused at several small towns long enough to allow some American passengers to disembark and new ones to climb aboard. I was too tightly wedged into my perch to reach my pack and my drawing pad. I contented myself with trying to commit all the sights to memory. We passed over several more bridges, and I could feel that we were starting to climb. In the mountains, the air was a little cooler, but it was dry and dusty. My throat was parched from the dust, smoke, and soot. At last we stopped at a camp. Off in the distance, I could see hundreds of tents clustered near some trees. At this hour of the day, the camp appeared nearly deserted. As soon as the train chugged to a stop, many of my countrymen rushed over to begin unloading the train. Several white men on horses rode back and forth, shouting orders.

We climbed off the Iron Dragon, stiff and sore from our cramped positions. The noise and the chaos were

confusing—the clang of iron, horses neighing, and men shouting many orders. One of the horsemen, seeing our bewilderment, galloped over and pointed us to some tables set near the tracks. My fellow travelers were already lining up before two men sitting there. A Chinese man stood beside them, translating for the newcomers. As each man approached, their name was entered in a ledger.

My father's group was first, and I learned that his group would camp nearby and work as graders. With shovels, picks, and wheelbarrows, they would dig away all plant life and rocks, making the roadbed perfectly level. The rocks they dug out of high spots would be used to fill in the low areas. When the roadbed was level and smooth, they would spread gravel. This raised the bed enough so that the rain would drain away and make it ready for the men who laid the rail. Our group was setting up a new camp several miles away. Hundreds of my countrymen were already a few miles away. They followed the surveyors, cutting down the trees along the route and hauling them to the sawmill, where they would be made into the crossties that would fit between rails. Our group's job would be to follow the tree cutters and cut and blast out the stumps ahead, making it ready for the graders.

Yi looked up at the tall trees surrounding us. "Everything is big in America—the men and even the trees."

Even though Yi was only four years older than me, no one questioned his age. His name was entered in the books, and at last it was my turn.

"I am Huang Chow, the headman," the translator said. "This is Mr. Strobridge and Mr. Crocker."

Mr. Strobridge had a black beard and a patch over one eye. I learned later that he had hurt it in a blasting accident. As I bowed low, there was some discussion among the men, and I heard the words I was beginning to recognize . . . *too young*.

"Please, venerable headman," I said quickly. "Tell Mr. Strobridge I am needed to help Zhang Wei cook the meals. I am a good worker and I am learning to speak English."

Huang Chow spoke briefly to the two men. "Mr. Strobridge wants to know what you know of the American language."

I thought quickly to my last lesson. "Head," I said, pointing. "Arm, hand, leg, stomach, back."

The other man at the table roared with laughter. My face turned red with shame, but Mr. Strobridge looked at me and nodded.

Huang Chow listened and then said, "Mr. Strobridge says to come see him when you have learned more. For now, you will help Zhang Wei in the afternoon. In the morning, you will be a mess attendant for the white workers." Although his words were polite, Huang Chow's

voice was no longer friendly. Perhaps he was ashamed that I had drawn attention to myself.

I bowed humbly and took my leave. My father's group was already helping to unload the boxcars, and there was no time to say good-bye. Some of the supplies were loaded on six packhorses, and we set off at a brisk walk, following a recently cleared, wide path through the woods.

It took several hours to reach our new home. Huang Chow walked at the head of the group. He walked at a fast pace even when the smooth path ended. Ahead of us a swath at least twenty-five feet wide had been cut through the forest, leaving hundreds of stumps.

The sharp crack of axes and the buzzing scrape of saws were the first indications we had reached the camp. In a large, rocky clearing, several large tents had been set up and the men were building crude shacks. Huang Chow instructed us to find space in the tents. "You will start work in the morning," he said.

"Hurry," Yi said quietly, coming up beside me. "Maybe we can get a space together."

Nodding, I followed him quickly to the largest tent. It was packed with cots and men were already claiming them, placing their belongings on top to show ownership. Yi and I found two cots together at the back of the tent. Leaving me to guard our place, Yi went back out. A few minutes later, he returned with two small wooden packing cases,

which he placed between our cots. "Our new home," he said, grinning.

We arranged our meager belongings and spread our sleeping mats on the cots. Yi stretched out on his and a minute later had fallen asleep. I was worried about the morning. I had no idea where I was to go to be a mess attendant for the white men.

I found Zhang Wei surrounded with boxes and bags carried in by the packhorses and mules, already hard at work setting up the cook tent. He gave me a nod, thinking I had come to help.

"I am glad to see you are a boy who takes his responsibilities seriously. Your father has taught you well. I need water," he said, handing me a pole with two kegs.

What could I say? I am not a responsible boy? I am a boy who wants to take a nap? I picked up the pole and headed where he pointed.

The river was on the other side of the stump-filled clearing. So was the white men's camp. Instead of tents there were several sturdy buildings. From the smells, I could guess which one was where I would work. A short distance away was a small blacksmith shop and another building where a man sat on a bench outside mending a harness. He scarcely looked my way as I hurried past, heading for the river.

The river was swift and cold. I had to climb a small embankment while balancing the heavy kegs. When I got back to camp, Zhang Wei directed me to dump the water into several large whiskey barrels and head back for more. By the time I got back from the fourth trip, I was ready to confess I was not a well-brought-up boy after all. This time, however, Zhang Wei told me to sit and handed me a small bowl of rice, cabbage, and tiny pieces of pork.

"The men will not be fed until tomorrow," Zhang Wei said. "But while they are resting, you and I have worked." Dishing himself up a bowl, he sat beside me.

"This is very good, Honorable Uncle," I said politely. "Have you been a cook a long time?"

Zhang Wei laughed. "I learned to cook by watching my wife. She was so beautiful. I liked to watch her when she prepared our evening meal. She sang while she worked. Like a nightingale."

I had never heard a man profess such love for his wife. My own mother and father were polite to each other, but never showed affection.

"Did she give you many sons?" I asked.

"Only one," Zhang Wei said. His face was suddenly dark. "There would have been many more, but the soldiers came and killed them both while I was away."

There had been a terrible war in the southern part of China for many years. It was called the Taiping Rebellion and millions of people had died. The government forces had finally won only a few years ago. We had been very fortunate. Soldiers had come to our house, but they had only taken our chickens and the last bag of rice my father was saving for seed.

"I am sorry to hear of your sorrow," I said. "I hope you will find them when you go to the other side."

Zhang Wei stood up. "A man should not burden a young boy with his troubles," he said. "Go to bed, Lee Chin. Tomorrow will be here too soon."

I bowed. "I am honored that you confided in me." I went to the tent and tried to sleep, but everything I'd seen that day whirled in my head, and I only dozed in fits and starts. It was not yet dawn when I stumbled out of the tent.

Zhang Wei was already up. He handed me a small bowl of rice and a cup of tea. "Eat quickly, young one. The workday starts at dawn, and the men have to be fed."

chapter four

I Go to Work

The white workers were already making their way to the mess cabin when I arrived. I thought they might be hostile. I should not have worried, however, because they all ignored me. I might as well have been a spirit.

The cook was the biggest man I had ever seen. He had an enormous stomach that fell over the top of his trousers and bounced when he walked. His head was nearly bald and a full beard covered most of his face. He would have been frightening if I had not noticed the smile crinkles around his eyes.

I bowed and pointed to myself. "Lee Chin," I said.

He pointed to himself, "Bossman." Then he handed me two kegs and pointed to the river. I looked for a pole, to help carry, but did not see one. Fortunately, the river was much closer to here than at our camp. By the end of the morning, the cabin was swept, water barrels filled, tables

polished, and pots and pans scrubbed. Bossman gave me an approving nod. His green eyes glittered above his wild red beard. I had never seen a man with red hair like his and I itched to draw him. He had watched me all morning as I patiently acted out his orders. I had added words to my American language, although I wasn't sure they would be very handy for conversation. "Get water, sweep floor, scrub pot." Maybe they would be useful when I got married, I thought, as I walked back to our camp. Although a good wife would know what was expected of her without being told. She would know also that her duty was to provide many strong sons. I thought of the American women I had seen on the ship and at the railway station. They did not seem to be bound by the traditions that had held the Chinese women for centuries.

"Take the tea," Zhang Wei said, as soon as he saw me. He poured hot tea into two kegs.

I balanced the kegs on the pole across my shoulders and headed to the work area. My countrymen were hard at work; I saw Yi leading a mule and a cart filled with chunks of tree roots and stones.

Suddenly, the foreman shouted, "Fire!" Everyone scurried behind trees. By the time I realized that I had walked right into an area where they were blasting out stumps, it was too late. There was a terrific "BOOM!" and large pieces of wood and rocks flew by my head.

The foreman did not notice, but Huang Chow was suddenly beside me. "Foolish boy, do you want to die?"

"No, Honorable Headman," I said. "I didn't know what was happening."

He glowered at me. "Fill the barrels quickly. It is past time for the men to have their tea."

I bowed and hurried over to the two whiskey barrels set off to one side. The kegs did not fill them up and I had to make the trip again.

When I got back from my second trip with the tea, Zhang Wei set me to work fetching water. As soon as they were done working, each man bathed and put on clean clothes before dinner. After dinner, most of the men gathered around makeshift tables made of shipping crates to play *fan-tan,* a simple game played by hiding buttons under a bowl and removing them four at a time. Then the players bet on the number remaining. Another game they liked was *pai gow,* played by scoring Chinese dominoes and gambling on the highest hand.

Yi found me while I was scrubbing the pots. "I was given the worst mule to pull my cart," Yi complained. "If I wanted him to go, he stopped. If I said stop, he went."

"Maybe he doesn't understand your dialect," I joked.

Yi seemed to consider the idea before he realized I was teasing. Then he smiled. "I know you were making a joke, Chin, but maybe it's true. I will ask the headman to find out

what the Americans say for *go* and *stop*." He hurried away on his errand and I finished up my tasks. The washtubs were emptied. The towels and dirty clothes were gathered up and the rice pots cleaned. I was too tired to do anything except stumble to my bed and fall asleep.

Each day was like the one before, but gradually my body got used to the work. Wu Chang resumed his lessons in speaking English for the few of us who were still interested. Most evenings I could barely stay awake, but I was determined to learn the Americans' language.

Every Sunday was our day off. The men still had to eat and there was still water to fetch and pots to scrub. Zhang Wei made sure I had some time off, however. Elder Cousin Yi often went with me to the river for a swim. I took my drawing book and sketched while Yi talked of home. Three Sundays went by and my father did not come to visit.

On the last Saturday night of the month, Mr. Strobridge galloped up, dirt and pebbles flying out from his horse's hooves. I was on my way to the river for one last load of water. I had to jump out of the way to avoid being run down. He had a big bag of gold coins. Huang Chow read off the names and made a mark in a ledger as the coins were counted out. When Strobridge had galloped off again, the headman sat down and men lined up for their pay. Huang Chow made careful notes in the ledger. Many of the men grumbled when they learned that they had to pay for the

shovels, carts, and other equipment. It too would be taken out of their pay a little bit at a time. Huang Chow carefully wrote down each man's payments. When it was my turn, I was dismayed by how little was left. There was money to pay for the passage we had borrowed, some to be sent to my mother, a dollar for the Six Companies, a dollar for Huang Chow to keep the accounts, and a dollar for my share of the food. When everything was done, I had only a few coins in my hand.

An idea had been growing in my mind. I was sure my father would send some money home to buy back Sunshine. I would save my money to help him. Surely, that would please him.

While I pondered this idea, Yi was looking glumly at his few remaining coins. I went to my cot to put the money in my bag. "The Americans don't know how to make proper coins," he said. "There is no hole in the middle to string them."

"They have little coin holders sewn into the inside of their trousers. They call them pockets," I said.

"We need a safe place to keep our money," Yi said. "Not every man is honorable."

I thought about the men who lost money gambling or spent all they had on a drug called opium. "We could ask Zhang Wei."

Zhang Wei found us two small cans for our money, and we hid them on a small cupboard made from a crate. On the top shelf was a small paper statue of a kitchen god. The shelf below was filled with spices. He put the cans behind the ginger and pepper.

"It is good that you save your money and not gamble it away like some," he said, with a dark look at two men squabbling over a gambling debt. "Winter is coming and you will need many warm clothes this high in the mountains."

Yi groaned. "I am never going to be a rich man."

"Patience, my young friend. Do you not have more now than you ever did in the Celestial Kingdom?"

Zhang Wei's wise words made us both feel better. "In a few months, when we have paid off our passage, we can save even more," I said.

All the way back to our sleeping quarters, Yi regaled me with tales of what he would do when he was rich. I envied him for knowing exactly what he wanted. I did miss home. I thought about our house. It was small but comfortable, with one large room for living. There was a small room for my parents, and another I shared with my brothers. Sunshine slept on her mat in the main room. Father had built a small courtyard outside the door, and my mother had planted pots of flowers to brighten the space. My father often sat at night with my uncles smoking their pipes. When my chores were finished, I sometimes sat

there sketching the hills and mountains we could see in the distance. It is warm there and, during good years, we could grow two crops of rice on the wetlands near the river. Then my father would carefully save seed for the next year and trade for a small pig to fatten. On the drier land, we grew cabbages and beans. Even though we only owned a few acres, until the drought, it kept us all fed. I knew my father hoped to earn enough money in America to buy more land now that my brothers were almost old enough to marry.

As much as I missed my home, there were so many interesting things in this new country. I wished I could travel around to see everything. I was still thinking on this when I fell asleep.

After my Sunday chores were done, I picked up my drawing book and color sticks, intending to spend the afternoon drawing. Then, just as I headed out of camp, I saw my father. His smile disappeared when he saw what I had in my hand. I bowed. "Honorable Father," I said respectfully. "I did not know you were coming."

"I hope you are working hard and not wasting your time with foolishness," he said, without a greeting.

"It is my day off, Honorable Father," I stammered.

Zhang Wei appeared from around the cook tent. "You have raised a fine son," he said. "No one could ask for a harder worker."

My father seemed surprised by the compliment, but he looked pleased. "This worthless one?" he said.

"He does the work of two men," Zhang Wei declared.

I was anxious to explain my duties. Perhaps Zhang Wei would allow me to fix a lunch to eat by the river. Before I could speak, my father looked over at some men starting a *fan-tan* game.

"I am glad to hear you are not a totally useless boy," he said absently. "I think I will join the game." With a short bow to Zhang Wei, my father left me standing there.

Zhang Wei gave me a sympathetic look. "Go and make your pictures," he said. "That game will not end soon."

Needing some company, I searched the camp for Yi. I finally spotted him sitting at a table, gambling with my father and his friends. I choked back my resentment. Only a few days ago, Yi and I had secretly made fun of the old men and their constant squabbling over the gambling games. It is not good to think ill of your father. Still, I could not help but wonder if he would like me better if I wasted my time gambling and bickering with the other men. I felt betrayed and was disappointed in Yi. How was he going to see his dream of being a wealthy man if he spent his time gambling?

I took my drawing pad and headed for the river. But as I crossed the trail that divided our camp from that of the white men, I was surprised to see a white boy about my age

sitting on a rock, reading a book. Smiling politely, I said in my best English, "How are you? My name is Lee Chin."

The boy was not much taller than me, but he was heavier. His face was red with sunburn and his nose had started to peel.

"You should wear a hat," I said. "Like mine."

The boy scowled. "All you John Chinamen look like girly men with your long braids and your silly-looking hats."

I knew I should walk away, but I could not help myself. "With curly red hair and tender skin, who is more like a girl?" I asked.

The boy's hands curled into fists and he started toward me. I took a fighting stance. Even though I knew I could get into big trouble fighting with a white boy, it seemed that I had no choice. His fist shot out straight toward my chin. I ducked, but not quite in time. His fist grazed the corner of my eye and along the side of my head. My twisting movement caught him off guard, however, and he staggered forward. At the same time, my foot struck out and tripped him. As he fell, he grabbed me and we fell to the rocky ground. Tumbling over, neither one of us got in many blows because, although he was heavier and stronger, I was wiry and tough from the weeks of carrying water and tea.

"Well, what is this?" a man said. Strong hands pulled us up, as though we weighed nothing.

The boy and I glared at each other. Several men had left the mess cabin and were hurrying over. Then I saw who it was holding us and my heart sank. It was Bossman. What if he fired me? If he told Huang Chow, the headman, my honorable father would be disgraced. Still, knowing all that, I wiggled, still angry and fighting to be free.

"By cracky, you've got more spunk than most of your kind," Bossman said, still holding tight. Several of the men mumbled, angry that I was fighting a white boy, although Bossman, surprisingly, seemed amused. "They are just being boys," he said mildly.

"We can't have no China boys attacking our children," one man said.

"I say we go tell Strobridge," said another.

"Wait," the boy said. He had been silent until now. "We were just playing. I asked him to show me some of that China fighting."

"Is that true?" one of the men asked.

"Sure it is," the boy said. "It was my idea."

Bossman let us loose finally and headed back to the cookhouse. The other men drifted away.

I looked at the boy. "Thank you," I said, with a bow.

"I ain't no snitch," he said. "That don't make me a friend neither." He started to walk away. My English was much improved, but I wasn't sure what "ain't no snitch" meant. I would have to ask Wu Chang. Suddenly, the

boy turned back. "You put up a pretty good fight for a pigtailed girl."

I started to get angry again until I realized he was teasing. "You fight good, too," I answered. "For a curly-haired girl."

I hurried back to our camp. Perhaps Father's game was finished and he was waiting for me. But he was still with his friends. I waited all afternoon. At least over dinner we would talk. But the gamblers merely waved at Zhang Wei for two bowls of rice, which they ate while they played. Zhang Wei watched them, but his face was passive and he did not comment. I went to bed at last, and when I arose the next morning, my father was gone.

chapter five

Lessons and Talking Wires

"**J**umping Jehoshaphat! Why didn't you tell me you could speak English, boy?" Bossman asked the next morning as I washed up the breakfast dishes.

"I am only just learning," I replied.

"Well, the best way to learn a language is to speak it. From now on we speak English in this kitchen. You come to me. Bossman, is it time to scrub the pots? Bossman, will you need more water for the day? It will be easier on me and you will be getting good practice. Do you understand, Lee?"

"My name is Chin," I said. "We Chinese say our family name first. I will do as you ask, Bossman," I replied, bowing slightly.

"That's another thing, Chin. No more bowing."

"As you wish, Bossman," I said, catching myself just before I bowed again. I wanted to ask him why, but I was afraid that would be impolite.

"Do you know what you are doing here?" Bossman asked suddenly.

"Earning money to send home," I said.

"No, I mean the railroad," he explained. "Sit down," he said, pointing to a table. On the back of a piece of paper, he drew a map. "This is America," he began. "All along the East Coast, the land has been settled a long time. The West Coast, not so long. The only way to get here is by wagon train and that takes months, or on a long journey by ship through dangerous waters. By train the trip will only take a few days. It will also open up all this area," he said, running his hand over the middle and western part of his map.

He went on to explain that there was a race between one company, called the Union Pacific, starting in the east, and our company, the Central Pacific, in the west. The government helped with financing and rewarded the companies with land grants. The Union Pacific did have hostile American Indian tribes to contend with, but it would be building on mostly flat land. The Central Pacific had the most difficult route because we were going straight through the mountains.

"It will be one of the greatest works ever done, and we are a part of it," he finished. I did not understand all of his words, but I understood enough to know we were part of something very important.

"Thank you for teaching me, Bossman," I said.

"I would like to learn more about your country," Bossman said.

I was surprised. An American who wanted to know about the customs in the Celestial Kingdom? Americans were full of surprises. "My country is very old," I began.

I was glad to have someone to talk with. I hardly saw Yi anymore. He worked several miles away on a big cut. He explained to me that this meant they were blasting through solid granite around a mountain or where the ground was too steep. He still worked with his mule, which he affectionately called Long Ears. He had to pay two dollars a month to use the mule, but it was better than carting the heavy rocks away with a wheelbarrow over the rocky ground. The rocks were used to fill in places where there were gaps. Other crews built trestles over the places too big to fill. Even from the camp, I could hear the steady "Boom! Boom!" of the blasts. Yi was hoping to become an explosives expert, but the headman said he was too young.

"There is really nothing to it," Yi said, on one of the rare days he was still awake when I got to the tent. "We are using over five hundred pounds of powder a day. Boom!" he added cheerfully.

"Not for me," I said. "Just the noise alone gives me a headache."

It was raining the next morning when I walked to the American camp. The roadbed was smooth; all the stumps

were removed and holes filled in. A line of gravel had already been spread, and across these the wooden boards. "Clang, clang, clang." From down the track I heard the sound of the rails being laid and I could not resist taking a few minutes to watch. A horse pulling a large wagon of rails came up the track. On each side, men pulled the rails loose. Bossman had told me each one weighed more than five hundred pounds. American workers pulled the rail free. At the foreman's command "Down," the rail was dropped into place. When the cart was empty, it was tipped over to allow another cart to pass them and then turned up again. In this manner they laid four rails to the minute.

Next came the gaugers, the spikers, and the bolters. They did three strikes to each spike, ten spikes to each rail. Working furiously, they laid four hundred rails to the mile. It was an exciting thing to watch and I wished to be part of a team like that instead of a cook's helper.

Suddenly, remembering my duties, I quickly raced to the cook shack, where I found Bossman in a cranky mood. "Jumping Jehoshaphat! You are late," he cried, boxing me across the shoulders. "If you can't be here on time, I'll find another helper."

"I'm sorry," I said contritely. "It won't happen again."

"By cracky, I said to stop that bowing!" he shouted.

I ran to fill up the water kegs. There were several tanks on one of the railcars, so it was an easier job than going to

the river. I ran past Mr. Strobridge's home. He was the only one who had his wife and children with him all the time. They lived in one of the railway cars, but Mrs. Strobridge had made it quite homey. There was an awning to make a porch and a canary cage hung outside the door.

Mrs. Strobridge was sitting outside under her awning. Beside her, several children sat at a table, writing. I wondered if they were being schooled. There was a girl writing along with the boys. A wave of sadness washed over me as I remembered my little sister, Sunshine, and her harsh life as a slave. She would never have the chance to learn to read and write. I was more determined than ever to help my father buy her back; I went to work almost forgetting that Bossman was not happy with me.

Bossman, however, could never stay mad for long. After a few minutes, he said, "I'm your boss. That means you owe me being on time and giving me a good day's work. I'm not one of your gods. You are a free man. You don't have to bow and act like I am. Do you understand? It makes most people in this country uncomfortable."

"I understand," I said. "But this is how we greet each other in China. It is a politeness like your people shaking hands. We Chinese bow a lot."

Bossman's booming laugh echoed around the cook shack. "Go on before you're late for your other job." I grinned at him. I liked this American very much.

Zhang Wei was making out a list of supplies for the next shipment when I arrived at our camp. "Better order warmer clothes," he said. "Winter comes early in the mountains. The ones who were here last year tell me that sometimes the supplies can't get through because of the mud and snow, so we need to order early."

I groaned. How would I ever save enough to help my father buy back Sunshine if I kept having to spend all my money? Still, I knew he was right. Although the days were still hot and dry, the higher altitudes would be much cooler.

The end of the track was now nearly ten miles past our camp and word came that we needed to move. Our camp's foreman would not let the men miss work to move the camp. There was a great bit of grumbling about this, and rightfully so, I thought. The American workers lived mostly in railroad cars. Although they were windowless and smelly, partially because the Americans did not bathe often, they were at least easy to move. Our camp was made up of tents, packing-case shacks, and dugouts. All this, including the cook-tent supplies, had to be carried by mules and carts and then set up again. It was a time-consuming, laborious job, and if it was done on Sunday, the men would lose their one day of rest, which they badly needed.

That night, when Mr. Strobridge came with our pay, Huang Chow spoke to him at length. The next morning,

slightly after dawn, I was amazed to see a locomotive and one car stop beside the camp. Boxes, kegs, tents, and even the crew were quickly loaded and we chugged our way to the new camp.

"I wonder how they got the word to send us the locomotive," I said.

"Through the wires," Yi said. "They can send messages that way. It runs all the way from Strobridge's office to Sacramento."

"They can talk over a wire?" I asked.

"Not really talk," Yi explained. "They make different sounds to match the letters in their writing. No one could ever make a voice go over a wire."

"I'll bet they can," I said. "If they can send sounds, I think someday they will send voices."

"I'll wager an American dollar," Yi said.

"Agreed," I said as we arrived at our new home.

chapter six

The Picture Box

One of Huang Chow's duties was to go ahead of us each time we moved and select a good site for a new camp. We worked our way past towns with strange names like Secret Town, Gold Run, and Dutch Flats. Near Dutch Flats, Huang Chow selected a good spot with tall pine trees along a river. I loved the smell of pines and the needles covering the ground. I decided that I liked the California mountains very much, with the cold, clear rivers and the scent of pine. Still, I would have given any number of mountains to be back home again.

The next Sunday I waited again for my father, but he did not come. Finally, I gave up and sat on a crate while Wu Ling shaved my head. He ran the razor over my forehead and the back of my neck so that only the small patch was left for the queue hair. The American men often made fun of our hairstyle, but all men in China wore their hair this way. It started when the Manchus conquered China and

started the Qing Dynasty two hundred years ago. Any man who did not wear his hair this way was considered disloyal. When the people refused, the Qing soldiers massacred thousands of men.

As usual, Wu Ling was grumbling, but it was such a nice day, I tried not to listen. Several other men were waiting their turn. Although Wu Ling was always grouchy, he was also very good at shaving heads so that the hair didn't pull on a dull razor.

The next morning, Zhang Wei told me we would be moving again at the end of the week. The new town was called Alta. Mr. Strobridge said this would be his winter quarters and settled his family into a house.

Zhang Wei was not happy with Huang Chow's choice for our new camp. "Look," Zhang Wei said, pointing to the bare hillside above us. "The mountain god gets angry when you cut down all the trees. It is a disaster waiting to happen."

"It is the best place that I could find. As usual, the Americans have the only good space," Huang Chow said with a sigh. "There are thousands of our countrymen camped in the area. We are lucky to find a level spot."

From where we stood, I could see the American camp. A short line of tracks called a spur had been built off the main line. On the spur were several bunkhouse cars, the cook car, and Mr. Strobridge's large office.

Several other buildings had been constructed, including barns for the horses and mules. Behind the camp the mountain was rocky and dotted with trees.

"We do all the work, and they get the best of everything. Even the mules are housed better than we are," Wu Ling complained.

The only other fairly flat spot for a camp was down an embankment of the road. "I will have dust from the road in my cooking when it is dry, and mud when it rains," Zhang Wei continued his grumbling.

"Then you find a better space," Huang Chow said crossly. "I see no better, but some are worse."

As far as the eye could see, every inch of ground was filled with my countrymen. Every locomotive arriving at the end of the track brought even more. I was no longer the youngest boy. I wondered if there were nothing but women left at home.

I helped Zhang Wei set up the cook tent and start the fires for tea and rice. When Zhang Wei said he didn't need me anymore, I wandered off to look around. I thought I might find my father and tell him how I was saving money to help him buy back Sunshine. Maybe at last he would be pleased with me.

As I walked down the tracks, I saw the man with the box; the one Yi said was making pictures. I stood politely waiting until the man finally emerged from under the cloth.

"Mr. McGee," I said, hardly believing it. Mr. McGee stared at me for an instant. "Lee Chin, the artist. You can speak English now."

I bowed. "This unworthy one is honored that you remember him," I said. "I have been learning your language, but I still have much to learn."

"Are you still drawing?" he asked.

"It is hard to find time," I answered truthfully. "But I have done a few."

"I would like to see them," he answered.

"I am most interested in your box," I said. "My cousin Yi said you can make pictures with it."

"That is true," Mr. McGee said. "It is called a camera. I am taking pictures to sell to magazines and newspapers. The American public is very interested in the building of this railroad." He motioned to a round piece with a glass in it. "Look in there. Tell me what you see."

I looked through the glass. There was our camp: the cook tent, sleeping tents, packing cases, kegs, barrels. And there was Zhang Wei starting fires for the evening meal.

I moaned. "What magic is this? Everything is on top instead of on bottom."

Mr. McGee laughed. "We say upside down. No magic. Would you like me to make a picture of you?"

"I would like that very much, Mr. McGee."

"Sit there," he said, pointing to a rock. He looked through his camera at me.

"Am I upside down?" I asked.

"You are indeed," he answered. "You must not move or the picture will be blurred."

"I will be as still as this rock I am sitting on," I promised.

"Good. Now stay there while I get the plate ready."

I noticed what looked like a small tent on wheels. Mr. McGee poured something thick and syrupy with a strange smell over a small glass plate. Then he dipped the plate in another solution. Keeping the plate covered, he quickly slipped it into his camera. A few seconds later, he hurried it back to his tent. "I am developing the picture now," he explained. "I have to do it in the dark. More light would ruin your picture."

Mr. McGee put the glass on a piece of thick paper and set it out in the sun.

"Now we wait a few minutes." He sat down on a rock. "I bring my son with me in the summer when he is out of school. He is about your age. I hoped he might be interested in taking pictures. It seems he is more interested in surveying. He is always pestering me for permission to go with the surveyors."

"I don't know this word," I said. "What kind of work does a surveyor do?"

"They go first and, with their instruments, they can find the best routes and map them out for the builders," he explained. "I suppose there will be a lot of work for them as the country opens up, measuring property lines and roadways. Still, a father likes his son to follow in his footsteps."

"My country is very old," I said. "We are required to honor our fathers and our fathers' fathers. A father can decide what a son is to do with his life. But Bossman says this is a new country, where people can try new things. He says if it wasn't like that, no one would have ever built this railroad."

Mr. McGee laughed. "In other words, I should let my son do what he wishes?"

"I am only a kitchen helper. It is not my place to tell you what to do," I said, alarmed that he would think me too bold. "My honorable father finds me a poor son because I would rather draw than be a farmer. Still, I can't stop wanting to draw. Perhaps it is that way with your son."

"I think you are very wise for your age," Mr. McGee said, as he stroked the long end of his mustache. He looked at the picture paper and handed it to me. I stared at the picture. "I am a very handsome fellow," I joked. "I will send this to my mother."

"I can make you another copy for yourself," Mr. McGee said. "That is the good thing about this new camera. With a

negative, I can make as many copies as I want." He put the glass on a new piece of paper and set it in the sun.

"I wish I could learn about your camera," I said.

"I am going back home to Sacramento tomorrow," Mr. McGee said. "But I will be back. Each time I come I will teach you a little."

I jumped up and bowed several times. "You are too kind, Mr. McGee."

"I am going to meet my son for dinner in town. Would you like to come, too?" Mr. McGee asked.

I hesitated. "Forgive me, Honorable Sir. I have seen your American food. Cow's flesh and potatoes. I cannot make a liking for it. At any rate, Zhang Wei will need my help soon."

Mr. McGee stuck out his hand. "Good-bye then, Lee Chin. I will see you when I get back."

I raced down the hill to our new camp. Zhang Wei was pouring vinegar and cloves over cabbage, and I could see small pieces of pork in the big iron pot. I sniffed in the savory smell. The foolish Americans did not know what good food was.

I showed Zhang Wei my picture. "Do you think that Huang Chow could ask the Six Companies to send this to my mother?"

"How did you get this?" Zhang Wei asked. He frowned the whole time I told him about Mr. McGee.

"It is not good to be so friendly with the foreign barbarians," he said. "I don't think you should show this to the headman. Ask Wu Chang to write a letter for you. Then slip the picture in the envelope before you seal it. You will have to pay Wu Chang. He teaches you English for free; you cannot expect him to do this for free, too."

His words were sharp and they stung with rebuke. "I would have known to pay Wu Chang," I said.

"I wonder if you are forgetting the old ways with all your time with the smelly ones," Zhang Wei said. "I think you must choose one side or the other. If the men grumbled that they want more money and might strike to get it, how can we trust that you will not tell your new friends?"

"I would not betray my own people," I cried.

Zhang Wei turned his back to me. "I am only telling you what others might think."

I was hurt and confused. How could Zhang Wei think I would betray my people? Was it so wrong to be friends with the white people? With a heavy heart, I picked up my pole and kegs to fetch water.

There were two huge tanks of water on one of the railcars on the spur. Just as I came around to the side with the spigots, a boy came running around the other side, knocking me down and sending the kegs rolling away. I scrambled to my feet.

"You again," the curly-haired boy sputtered. "Can't you heathens watch where you're going?"

I fought to control my temper. I bowed. In my language I said, "You are a horse's hind end. You are ugly and you smell. You are so rotten even the wild dogs would turn up their nose." Then in English I said, "I am sorry, Honorable Young Sir. I should have watched where I was going."

His eyes narrowed suspiciously. "What are you trying to pull?"

"I do not understand you. Did I not say it was all my fault?" I said, looking innocent.

"We both know it was my fault. That's what I hate about you Chinamen. Always bowing and smiling, and I know you can't mean it." He paused. "I get it. When you were talking your talk you were telling me off but good, right?"

I did not answer, and after a minute he said, "I'm late. I'm supposed to meet my dad for dinner." He raced away, but I stared after him with shock. I knew who that curly-haired boy was. He was Clay McGee's son.

chapter seven

Mudslide

It was raining the next morning. My mood was as gray as the cloudy skies. I did my work for Bossman, saying nothing more than needed to be said. Several times I caught him watching me while I worked, but I pretended not to see. All morning I fought with myself. I knew that most of my countrymen did not trust the Americans. They were there to do a job, collect their money, and go home. And many Americans were not nice. I remembered the taunts of the crowd in San Francisco. Still, I had met two Americans that I liked very much.

Bossman had been telling me about a war that had just ended in America. I wanted to hear more.

After the last pot was put away, I poured Bossman a cup of the coffee he preferred over tea. Bossman scratched his beard and gave me a long look. "So what's bothering you this morning?" he asked.

"I am sorry, Bossman. I had some thinking to do. But I have figured out a way to solve my problem." This was not

exactly true. I had decided to hide my problem. I would not mention any conversations with my American friends to anyone, not even Elder Cousin Yi. This way, I would maintain the trust of my people and still keep my new friends.

"You were telling me about the war," I said quickly, not wanting him to ask any more questions. "Why did the Americans fight each other?"

"The southern states wanted to keep slaves to work on their big plantations. People began to realize how terrible slavery was, but the southern states decided to make their own country. We couldn't allow that. If a state left the union because it didn't like something or other, soon there would be no country left. So I, like a lot of the men you see here, marched off to war."

I sat up straighter. "You were a soldier, Bossman?" I had been taught that soldiers were all bad people. In my country both the Taiping and the government soldiers had slaughtered civilians. I tried to reconcile that with the Bossman I knew. Although he was big and perhaps a little scary looking, I knew he was like a gentle giant. He was seldom angry and often I saw the men come to him for help or advice

"War is always terrible," Bossman said. "But some things are worth fighting for. I fought for the Union, but many of the men you see here fought for the Confederacy.

This country still has a lot of healing to do. Building this railroad may help bring us together again."

"There is slavery in China," I said.

"Then, when you go home, you must do what you can to change it," Bossman said.

"China is a very old country," I said. "We are a country of traditions. Slow to change. At any rate, war, droughts, and floods cause terrible famines. People sell themselves or their children to keep them from starving."

Bossman looked at me. "That is very sad."

I did not tell him my father had sold my little sister. I just nodded.

It was still raining as I walked back to our camp. The dry earth was turning into slippery mud. I tried to jump from one clump of grass to another to keep from sliding. I thought about Bossman's words as I walked. He had given me a lot to think about.

Zhang Wei was in a bad mood from the rain. "I have had a terrible time keeping the cooking fires burning," he complained as he pointed to the tiny streams of water making little gullies in the ground. I filled up the tea kegs and balanced the pole across my shoulders.

I was the one who should be grumbling, I thought as I trudged up the slippery slope. At least Zhang Wei could stay dry in the cook tent.

Yi was the first one to the tea containers. "I have not seen you for a long time," I said. "It seems the only times we can talk, one of us is sleeping."

"We are going to start working on a tunnel soon," Yi said, keeping a watch out for the foreman. "I have asked the headman if I could learn to work with explosives. They say there is a new kind of explosive. It's called nitroglycerin and everyone says it is very safe to handle. It is a good time for me to learn. After all, when it is New Year, I will be seventeen."

For centuries it has been a tradition that all Chinese people celebrate their birthday on the New Year. "I will be thirteen," I reminded him.

"You are still a baby," he teased. Seeing the foreman coming, he drained his cup and headed back to his work, filling up the cart with rocks from the blasting.

"Get to work," the foreman shouted to Huang Chow, who had just come for his tea. "Tell the rest of your yellow apes we have a race to win. The Union Pacific workers do not stop for tea every few hours."

All of the white people talked about the race. It did not seem like a fair race to me. Bossman said the Union Pacific was building across mostly flat land. We had to build eleven tunnels through hard rock.

That night I relaxed by the fire for a few minutes before going to bed. The rain had stopped but there was a chill in

the air, and I was glad my new quilted winter clothes had arrived in the last shipment. In spite of the cold, it was a pleasant evening. The dinner pots were scrubbed, the bathwater dumped, and the towels picked up. Some of the men were already asleep. A few old men sat by the fire with their water pipes.

I thought of home before the famine. In the evening, when we came in from the fields, I would draw while my brothers wrestled outside the door. Sunshine would sit in the corner of the kitchen playing with the doll my mother had made for her out of cloth and stuffing. My father had been very disappointed that my mother had given him a female child. He hardly ever spoke to Sunshine. I was the one Sunshine came to if she skinned herself or bumped her head. I wondered if she understood that I could not help her now, or if she thought I had deserted her.

Huang Chow sat beside me and picked his teeth with an ivory toothpick. After a few minutes, he turned to me. "How is your job with the Americans? Do the men treat you well?"

"My job there is almost the same as here, Honored Sir," I answered truthfully. "The men ignore me. They don't even call me names. They just act like I don't exist."

Huang Chow looked pleased. "It is better that way. The Americans do not understand our ways. They make no

attempt to learn our language, but expect us to learn theirs. They want us to accept their ways, but we will not."

I wondered what would happen if the Americans went to the Celestial Kingdom. Would we not expect them to accept our ways and learn our language? I kept these thoughts to myself.

After a minute Huang Chow went to bed.

When I stepped out of the tent the next morning, the sky was filled with tiny white flakes, so thick you could hardly see. I had never seen snow before. I knew that most of the workers dreaded it, but I thought it was quite wonderful. I stuck out my tongue and captured the flakes on it. I watched my footprints as I walked to the American camp.

"I see you are in a better mood today," Bossman said as I burst through the door, stamping the fresh snow off my boots.

"I didn't know snow was so beautiful," I said.

"By cracky, tell me how beautiful you think it is in a couple of months," he laughed.

By afternoon, the snow had melted and it was raining again. The rain continued for the next three days. For each day it rained, tempers grew shorter. It was difficult to walk. With each step, I sank into the mud so that it took me twice as long to deliver the tea. The men griped at me. "Lee Chin, did you stop for a picnic on the way? Tell Zhang Wei to get someone who is strong enough to walk through a little mud."

I walked back to camp feeling alone and sorry for myself. Zhang Wei scolded me. "What took you so long?" Without waiting for my answer, he said, "Get the water heating for baths." Silently we worked, getting ready for the crew's return. I worked fast, and when the first of the crew arrived, everything was ready. Zhang Wei smiled. "Good," he said.

Suddenly, there was a rumbling noise in the bare hillside above us and the ground seemed to slump. I looked up to see a wall of thick, black mud sliding toward the camp.

There was no time to run. The mud swept us off our feet. It oozed thickly down the hill, carrying rocks, small trees, men, tents, and belongings along with it. I fought to keep my face out of the slippery mud. In a panic, I tried not to think what it would be like to drown in mud, to feel mud filling your lungs. Some of the men were screaming, but I was too frightened to make a sound. Then, just as quickly as it had started, it was over. I struggled to stand, but the heavy mud sucked at me, pulling me down. The mud was nearly to my waist. Some of the workers from the next camp had heard the screams and came to help. Someone threw me a rope. I grabbed it gratefully while two men dragged me to solid ground. Every inch of me was covered in mud.

I looked around in disbelief. A few minutes ago, there had been a crowded camp, but now there was only mud. Here and there the remains of a tent or a crate poked out.

The cook tent was still standing. I looked for Zhang Wei. He was desperately trying to save the food barrels. The mud had stopped just short of the cook tent, and Zhang Wei's dinner was safe. Zhang Wei pointed to the kitchen god sitting serenely on his shelf in the cook tent. "We must send a prayer of thanks," he said.

The rest of the camp had not been spared, however. The bathtubs and clean clothes were gone. The crates where the men sat to play their games were crushed and buried. The big tent had collapsed and smaller ones were completely gone.

Huang Chow, covered with mud like everyone else, walked to Mr. Strobridge's office to report what had happened. I thought maybe Mr. Strobridge would send some of the Americans to help us, but instead he set them to work clearing the tracks, which were deeply buried. A short time after Huang Chow returned, I saw Bossman driving a wagon. On it was one of the big water tanks.

Huang Chow bowed deeply. "Tell Mr. Strobridge we thank him."

Bossman caught my eye, and I thought he was going to speak. Quickly, I bowed.

Bossman seemed to understand my position. "I will still expect you on time for work in the morning, Lee Chin," he said gruffly.

I bowed again. "I will be there, Bossman."

Standing nearby, Huang Chow and Zhang Wei had watched this conversation with interest. I saw them exchange a look and knew that they had discussed my friendship with Bossman.

Bossman drove the wagon away, but a few minutes later, he returned with a shovel. Although Huang Chow protested, saying we did not need help, Bossman insisted on staying. He worked tirelessly for hours as we repaired the camp.

Most of the men who had been caught in the mud went to the river to wash off the worst of it in the icy water. When I returned to camp, I saw that men from other camps had brought tubs and were already digging out what could be saved from the mud. Working together, we soon had the camp almost restored. Although the big tent had collapsed, very little mud actually got inside. Men shoveled around the tent and set it up again. The smaller tents were pulled out of the mud and washed off. New water was heated for baths, which were badly needed now. Most of the clothes and belongings were found, washed, and set out to dry.

The packing crates that we used for tables and chairs were gone, but Zhang Wei assured the men that he would have more the next day. The men stood or squatted to eat their meal. Some of the men complained while they ate.

"What will prevent this from happening again?" they asked. But the main worry was about the coming winter.

"We will not survive in these flimsy tents. We need better housing," one of them said.

"You must talk to Mr. Strobridge," all the men told Huang Chow.

Huang Chow looked uncomfortable. I knew that he did not like confrontation. "It is in our contract that we provide our own housing."

"It is not right," Wu Ling said loudly. "The Americans get all the good jobs. Do you see any of us being made a foreman, or even a tracklayer? We do all the hard work. The Americans make more money and they get their board. We should strike."

"That is not our way," said Huang Chow. "I wish to hear no more of that talk."

Wu Ling would not be quieted. "The old ways were good for the Celestial Kingdom. They are not good for here. The Americans call us names and we just smile and bow."

"What do you think of Wu Ling's ideas?" I asked Yi, when we went to bed.

"Stay away from him," Yi said. "He's a rebel. His ideas will get us all in trouble."

I did not tell Elder Cousin that I believed Wu Ling was right.

chapter eight

Nitroglycerin

Fortunately, the rains seemed to be over. Day after day dawned, cool, but bright and sunny. A breeze dried up the mud and everyone's sprits seemed high. Some of the men even built a joss house.

"A joss house sounds something like a church," Bossman said, when I told him about it. "But of course the Americans only have one god," he told me.

"I have heard that before but it seems like a strange idea. In China we have many gods," I bragged.

"What do you do in a joss house?" Bossman asked.

"In the Celestial Kingdom some of the joss houses are very big and beautiful. Some of them have statues of the gods, and when you go in you can burn a joss stick for the gods or your ancestors."

The joss house at camp was little more than a shack. There were no statues, although someone had placed a

small, beautiful ceramic bowl on the shelf and there were often colorful wildflowers from the hills. Soon the walls were covered with lucky symbols painted on paper. Men paid Wu Chang to draw them.

The talks with Bossman helped me learn English, and Bossman also taught me the numbering system and how to write. It was much easier to learn the American writing, with a sound for each symbol. Chinese writing is much more complicated. It takes years to learn because there are thousands of characters. Each one is made precisely with the correct number of strokes, so that it is like a fine work of art.

When Wu Chang wrote the letter to my mother, I did not tell my mother that I was learning to write the American way. I also did not mention the slowly growing fund to buy my sister. I wanted to tell my father of my secret plan first. But I had not seen him since early summer. I made up my mind to find his camp and tell him my plan.

I dictated my letter, telling her about my work and how much I missed her. I asked her if she had seen Sunshine or heard any news about her. When I was finished, I paid Wu Chang a dollar for his help.

"It is a fine letter," Wu Chang said. He folded a paper envelope and I slipped the picture inside. Then Wu Chang sealed it with melted wax. The next day I gave the letter to

Huang Chow. He promised to put it in the mail pouch that went to the Six Companies office in San Francisco each week. I knew it would be a long time before the letter reached my home.

"Your mother will be happy to hear from you," Huang Chow said. "You are young to be away from home. I hope you do not have to wait long for an answer."

"Thank you, Honored Sir," I said.

Huang Chow waved me away. He had looked distracted for several days. Wu Ling had continued talking to the men, and now many of them were complaining to Huang Chow. Although the weather was still good, everyone knew that winter was coming, and the higher we went up the mountain, the worse it would be.

Yi wasn't happy with Huang Chow either. The head-man had told Yi he was too young and too impatient to work with the explosives. Yi sulked for several days, but his natural good humor eventually won out.

"The nitroglycerin is much more powerful than the black powder," Yi told me. "They make a line of holes and pour it in. Boom!" Yi made his hands fly up in demonstration.

Bossman had another side of the story. "They have been using five hundred pounds of black powder a day," he said. "The nitro is new and people say it is safe to handle. There have been some accidents, though. One of the

warehouses in New York blew up for some unknown reason, and there was a big explosion in San Francisco. I have heard that Mr. Crocker and Mr. Strobridge are concerned about using it, even though it makes the work go twice as fast. Your cousin might be luckier than he thinks not to use it."

I was going to tell Yi what Bossman had told me that night, but I never got the chance. Shortly after I started my job with Zhang Wei, several men from the crew ran into the camp.

"There has been a terrible accident. Several men have been killed. The new explosive."

I only had one moment to enjoy a feeling of relief knowing that Yi was not allowed to work with explosives before I noticed one of the men giving me a pitying look. My legs gave out and I sank to the ground. Zhang Wei led me to a crate chair and put a cup of tea beside me.

"Not Yi," I moaned. "He was always happy. He was going to get very rich and go home and marry two wives. He was going to have a happy life in the Celestial Kingdom. How can it be, when he was not permitted to handle the explosives?"

Finally, one of the men told me what had happened. "One of the charges did not go off, but no one noticed. One of the men from another crew struck it with his pick and it exploded. Several men were working nearby, picking up

rocks to fill their carts. Three men from the other crew were killed and also Lee Yi and Wu Ling."

My mind would not accept the news. Surely, it was some terrible mistake. Surely, at any second, Yi would pop in front of me and say, "Oh, Little Cousin, what a sad thing for you to have to worry."

But Yi did not appear to say those words and, a few minutes later, a cart arrived with the bodies of Yi and Wu Ling. My father walked solemnly beside it, his eyes downcast. As Yi's uncle and closest relative, my father would arrange the funeral.

There was a great deal of discussion between my father and Huang Chow. Mr. Strobridge gave permission for the bodies to be taken by train to Sacramento, where the agent for the Six Companies would arrange a proper funeral and burial in the Chinese cemetery. Later, they would ship their bones back to the Celestial Kingdom.

Two wooden coffins were hastily constructed. Some of the men wrote letters to family members who had died, and put them in the coffins, hoping that Yi and Wu Ling would give the messages to their loved ones when they reached the other side.

When the locomotive was ready, we formed a long procession to carry the coffins to the train. My father and Huang Chow would accompany the bodies and return the

next day. My father was very distraught and said little to anyone. Yi had been his favorite nephew.

The rest of us followed, chanting a song to confuse any devils that Yi or Wu Ling might have offended and might be following to take revenge. We wanted to get them confused so they didn't know which way the bodies had gone. Zhang Wei had cooked many fine dishes and brought new clothes. That way, when the ancestors came to lead Yi and Wu Ling to the other side, they would find the supplies for the long journey.

As the bodies were loaded on the railcar, all of us took small squares of brightly colored paper and folded it. Then we tore a tiny, round hole in the center and threw the papers to the wind. We did this until the train pulled away. We believed that any remaining devils would have to make themselves very small to get through the tiny holes and that would leave them trailing farther behind. After awhile they would get so discouraged that they would forget their need for revenge.

Back at camp, Zhang Wei bustled around me like a mother hen. He offered me a bowl of rice with tasty pieces of pork and vegetables. I nibbled at it to please him, but it churned in my stomach.

My father and Huang Chow returned the next afternoon. Zhang Wei insisted that my father eat with us before

going back to his camp. I knew he did it for me so that my father and I would have a chance to talk.

I handed my father a bowl. "Zhang Wei makes good dumplings," I said.

"I had the agent write a letter to Yi's mother," my father said. "It will be difficult for her. First my brother dies and now his oldest son."

He ate in silence for a few minutes. "Zhang Wei does indeed make good dumplings. He has given me praise for rearing such a hardworking son."

"This one is unworthy of all his praise," I said. "I only do my job like everyone else."

I took a deep breath. "I have been wanting to talk to you, Honorable Father," I said. "I had a wonderful idea and I have been saving money for it."

My father gave me a curious look. "What is your idea, Chin?"

I told him of my savings to help him buy back Sunshine. Instead of a pleased expression, his face darkened with anger.

"Foolish boy! The worthless girl was sold to a wealthy family. She will work for them, and later they might arrange a marriage for her. If you bring her back, I will have another mouth to feed and, in a few years, I will have to pay for her to marry. I am the father. I will make these

important decisions. We will not buy her back. I forbid you to even mention this again!"

He stormed off to talk and gamble with his friends. I stared after him, stunned by his anger. I had managed to convince myself he planned on buying back Sunshine and would be grateful for my help. How could I have been so foolish?

I did not see him again before he left. Someone had already taken Yi's cot. I lay awake for a long time, listening to the snores and dreaming murmurs of the sleeping men around me, and thinking about Yi, Sunshine, and my father.

chapter nine

Missouri Bill
and the Locomotive

Mr. Strobridge and Mr. Crocker rode into camp to announce that we would not be using the nitro again.

Huang Chow bowed. "The men will be very happy to hear that, Honorable Sirs."

"The men will have to work hard, though," Mr. Strobridge said. "The Union Pacific is ahead of us."

"I will give them your message," Huang Chow said, bowing again.

That night at dinner, Huang Chow delivered Mr. Strobridge's message. "Did you ask him about more money?" one of the men called out. He was a young man and I knew he had been friends with Wu Ling.

"They will not agree to that," Huang Chow said.

I looked up from my bowl of rice. Huang Chow did not know that I had been close enough to overhear the conversation. I knew that he had not mentioned more money.

Some of the men grumbled, but without Wu Ling to work them up, they soon went back to their dinner.

The men who worked with explosives were happy to go back to black powder, even though it was slower work. More and more workers came from China. One of the men told me that there were more than seven thousand Chinese working for the Central Pacific. Twice a day, when I carried the tea, I passed camp after camp along the way. There were not enough tents for the newcomers, and some of them had simply dug a hole for their sleeping mats and covered it with a small piece of canvas for protection from the cold. There were so many workers you could hardly walk without stepping on someone's belongings. It was raining again, a cold, stinging rain that made my face red and chapped, and soaked right through my clothes.

Word came that some of the crews were being sent to the long tunnel at the summit. Some other crews were sent to the other side of the tunnel to work toward the crews on the west end of the tunnel. Still, others were sent to grade for the track in a place called Truckee. Our crew would stay here and work on tunnels one and two so the rail could reach a town called Cisco.

Mr. Crocker said he wanted crews working on the tunnels twenty-four hours a day. The men worked eight-hour shifts, which made it even harder for Zhang Wei to have hot meals for everyone.

The men continued to gripe until Huang Chow finally worked up his courage and went to talk to Mr. Strobridge about housing. When he came back, Huang Chow looked smug. "Mr. Strobridge says there are cabins we can use while we build the tunnels. He has had crews working all summer to build housing by the summit tunnel."

The work on the cuts and tunnels was brutal. One man held the drill and another hit it with a heavy sledgehammer. The rocks were so hard that a new drill had to be used every few inches. When a hole was big enough, it was packed with black powder. The fuse was lit and the workers ran to get out of the way. Sometimes, however, the rock was so hard that the powder just blew out. Even working as hard as they could, the men were only able to clear a foot a day. Mr. Strobridge walked around, barking orders. He was a big, formidable man and his presence made everyone work harder.

With three shifts to feed, my work was harder, and I seldom had time to myself. One Sunday, Zhang Wei insisted I take a few hours off. I wandered away from the camp, trying to decide what to do with my rare free time. Then, on a small hill near our camp, I saw a familiar face. Clay McGee was setting up his camera. A few feet away was his developing tent on a small cart with wheels.

"Lee Chin," he called. "I was wondering if I would see you again. I have been looking for you, but there are so many of your people now."

I bowed. "I am happy to see you, Mr. McGee. I also have been looking for you. Are you taking pictures today?" I asked.

Clay McGee nodded. "Would you like to help?'"

"I would be honored to help, Mr. McGee, sir."

"Good. Look through the lens and set it in place for a good picture. A good photographer must have a good eye for a scene. If the picture is too busy, people will not understand what they are looking at. On the other hand, if there is not enough, they may find the picture boring. You need to look at the front of your view. Is there a big rock cutting off a corner? And the back. Is there an odd-shaped object that throws the picture out of balance?"

While he talked I looked through the camera lens. Off to one side was the cut. Carts were lined up, waiting for the workers in the morning. That would be a better picture tomorrow when the men were working. I swung the lens over our camp. Men were washing clothes, gambling, or sitting with their pipes. Then I saw it. At the animal barns, an American was trying to harness one of the mules to one of the carts. The man was determined to have his way, but the mule was just as determined to have his. The man pulled and the mule laid back his ears and dug in, pulling back so hard he was almost sitting.

"Hurry with the plate," I said. "I don't know how long this picture will last."

Mr. McGee must have seen it, too, because he came running with the plate and slipped it in. Hoping I had aimed the lens correctly, I stepped back. Mr. McGee counted, "One, two, three, four, five, and six."

I followed Mr. McGee as he moved quickly to the developing tent. Holding my plate by the edge, he poured the developer across the picture. "It has to be very quick and very smooth or you will have ridges and lines. It takes some practice."

"Now watch," Mr. McGee said. It was dark, but I could see dark places and lighter spaces that slowly became a recognizable picture. "Looks like we have a good one."

"We have to leave the developer on just the right amount of time. If it is left on too long, the image will get cloudy. Now we wash it," he said, pouring water over every inch of the picture.

"It is very difficult," I said. "I am not sure I will be able to remember everything."

"Mostly, it just takes practice," he said. He showed me how to fix the picture with a mixture of potassium cyanide and then wash the picture again.

"These are dangerous chemicals," Mr. McGee warned. "They can catch fire and they can make you sick. Promise me you will not touch them unless I am with you."

I bowed. "You have my promise."

Mr. McGee dried the photograph by moving a small alcohol lamp across the picture. "Good. Now here is something you may like." He handed me a small brush and box of dry color.

"Just a touch of color," he said, pointing. "The man's hands and cheeks. Then, when you are done, we will put a sealer on it for protection."

I bent over my work, carefully applying color as he suggested. I added a bit of color to the mule's long ears. I considered several other places but decided against them. The picture looked perfect to me already. I blew off the excess color and looked up to see Mr. McGee watching me intently.

"It is a good picture, is it not?" I asked.

"It is very good. I think you have found your calling," he said. "Maybe when you go back home you can open a photography shop. Do you think there are photographers in the Celestial Kingdom?"

I nodded. "My Elder Cousin had seen one before we left for America."

"I heard about your cousin. I am very sorry, Lee Chin."

"Elder Cousin is with the ancestors on the other side. I will see him again when it is my time to die."

I helped Mr. McGee clean up his developing tent and carefully stored the chemicals. As we worked he told me a little about each one. Finally, he stopped. He took off his hat and ran his fingers through his thick hair. "Heck, Lee Chin.

I'm not going to be able to teach you everything you need to know. You need to be an apprentice. If you were not going home as soon as the railroad was done, I could take you in my shop and teach you."

"I will think on that," I said, bowing.

"Then it's a deal. If you decide to stay, you will work for me," he said, sticking out his hand in that strange way Americans have. I was used to it now, though, and it did not bother me. I put my hand in his and we shook.

"Wait a minute," he said. "I have an idea. The Central Pacific is bringing a stripped-down locomotive to the summit to use as a hoist. They brought it to Colfax, and from there a muleskinner named Missouri Bill is going to bring it on a specially built wagon to the summit. It should be quite a sight and I am hoping to get some good pictures. I could use a helper. Do you think you can get off work for two days?"

I shook my head. "I have never missed work," I said. "I don't know what they would do without me."

"I will talk to Crocker. Maybe we can find someone to take your place. Heck, I would pay their wages."

I did not say anything when I returned to my camp. I delivered the tea and started my evening chores, all the time keeping an anxious watch for Mr. McGee. I did not have to wait long. Just as I sat down to eat, Mr. Crocker galloped into our camp.

Huang Chow hurried over to speak to him. He looked surprised as he motioned for me to come.

"I have a job for you, boy. I am told you speak English."

I bowed. "I am still learning, Honorable Sir."

Mr. Crocker laughed. "You are the boy who named the body parts. Well done. You have learned a lot since then. Maybe you will be a headman someday."

Huang Chow frowned at this. I quickly bowed. "There is much more to being a headman than just speaking English. I have seen all the things Huang Chow has to do. He keeps everyone's working hours and money to the Six Companies to be sent home, and each man's share for Zhang Wei's food order."

Huang Chow held up his hand. "Enough, Lee Chin," he said. "Mr. Crocker has come to ask for your help, not hear a list of my qualities." To Mr. Crocker he said, "Lee Chin is very young. I have many good men."

"The photographer asked for Lee Chin. He wanted someone who spoke English. You do, but you are needed here with your crew. Find someone to take the boy's place for two days. You be at the end of the track at first light," Mr. Crocker said, as he galloped away.

I could hardly sleep for my excitement. Zhang Wei and Huang Chow had both given me a long talk.

"Do a good job," they said, "but do not listen to their ideas. The old ways are best."

The next morning, Mr. McGee was already waiting for me. At the end of the track was a locomotive that sat on a huge, round metal plate. We watched as men turned the roundtable until the locomotive was turned around and headed for Sacramento. From a short spur, several waiting cars were hooked on and we were ready to go. I helped Mr. McGee stow the developing tent and a box with carefully measured chemicals in a boxcar. Then I followed him to the passenger car.

"Am I allowed?" I asked nervously.

Mr. McGee held up a ticket. "You have paid your fare."

We sat down and Mr. McGee let me take the window seat, although he said there was too much smoke and cinders to open them. Several men got on, but they did not seem to notice me. I settled back in the seat, which was covered with a rough, itchy cloth, and watched the miles fly past.

At last, we reached Colfax. Mr. McGee had arranged to rent a horse and wagon there. We loaded our supplies and headed off. We had not traveled very far when the horse began prancing nervously and his eyes rolled up in terror. A man ran toward us. "Blindfold your horse if you are going past," he shouted.

Suddenly, we could hear why the horse was so nervous. From not far away came a rumble of wooden wheels, the bawling of oxen, and the clank of chains. Above everything

else I heard the crack of a whip and a man's booming voice. We tied the rented horse in a grassy spot off the road and walked toward the noise.

I will never see such a sight again in my life. The engine was mounted on a huge wagon pulled by ten yoke of oxen. The wheels on the wagon were two feet wide. The trail at this point sloped down. Missouri Bill and his helpers put a log stop under the wheels. Then they attached a heavy chain to the nearby trees on each side of the road, leaving just a little slack when they fastened it to the wagon. Then Missouri Bill kicked away the log brakes, allowing the wagon and the engine to slide forward a few feet. Then the process would be repeated.

"If they didn't do it that way, the weight of the engine would make it impossible to stop. He will do the same thing in reverse when he is going uphill to keep it from rolling back," Mr. McGee said. "He has seventy miles of trails to cover and he has promised to deliver the engine in six weeks."

"Do you think he will make it?" I asked.

"Strobridge and Crocker hired him, so they must think he can."

Mr. McGee was anxious to get to work while the sun was high and bright. Good light was the most important thing for a quality picture. We could not ask Missouri Bill to hold still for his picture so we decided to set up in front

of him so we would be ready when he came by. We found a likely spot and worked furiously to be ready. We could hear the rumble of the wagon crashing through the woods and the bawling of the oxen long before we could see him. I had aimed the camera where I thought he would be. I hoped I was right, because there was no chance to change it now.

"Ready," I yelled as the engine came into view.

Mr. McGee hurried out with the prepared plate. Missouri Bill stood up and cracked a long whip over the oxen. Mr. McGee pulled the dark cover off the plate. "One, two, three, four, five, six," we counted together.

The picture was good, caught at the very moment Missouri Bill's whip snapped in the air.

"Let's try to get another picture," Mr. McGee said, pushing the developing cart to a spot overlooking the trail. We hurried forward again and, in this way, we had three good pictures to take back. Mr. McGee was ecstatic. "You brought me good luck, Lee Chin. I can sell all three of these pictures."

I grinned happily. His words made me feel very proud. I studied the first picture as we rode the train back to my camp. "I want to draw this," I told Mr. McGee.

"I hope I can see it," Mr. McGee said when we arrived. "Remember to think about staying in this country, at least for a time. I think you could have a bright future here."

"I will," I promised. We shook hands in the American way, and I ran back to camp with a happy heart.

Huang Chow was waiting for me. "Why did the American ask for you?" he asked, frowning.

"It was hard work, climbing up and down with a wagon. You are too important and needed here. I was the least important member of the crew," I said.

Huang Chow considered my answer. "Do not let all this time with the Americans make you forget the old ways. The Americans are barbarians. They do not understand our ways," he said, as he waved his arm. "Go to Zhang Wei, but do not forget what I say."

I bowed low. "I will not forget, Honorable Headman."

Zhang Wei was happy to see me. "I did not realize how helpful you are," he said. "That one who took your place had to be told everything. Empty the bathwater, pick up the towels, and stir the cabbage. I even had to send him back three times to get the rice pot clean."

It was nice to feel important.

chapter ten

Avalanche!

I was too excited from my adventure to sleep that night. I lay awake, listening to the snores of the other men and thinking about Mr. McGee's offer. All this time I had been yearning to return home, and yet, if I did, I would become a farmer like my father and brothers. Yet how could I defy my father and stay? Was Huang Chow right? Was I forgetting the old ways? I had not decided when I fell into an uneasy sleep.

It was snowing when I stepped out of the tent the next morning, and it was bitterly cold. I was grateful that Zhang Wei had insisted I spend part of my savings on a padded jacket and trousers. At first I was delighted with the snow, although the other men grumbled. On the way to work for Bossman, I stuck out my tongue and let the snowflakes melt on my tongue. But the snow kept on falling without stopping for the next three days. When it finally did stop, there was nearly three feet of snow on the ground. I could

hardly make it to my jobs each day. Although part of the crew was put to work shoveling, it was a powdery snow that drifted right back with the wind.

Zhang Wei offered me some snowshoes, but the snow was too soft even for them. In spite of the snow, the work went on. Mr. Strobridge was anxious to get the end of the track to Cisco, a town that lay 5,900 feet high and only a few miles from the summit. A lot of crews were already working at the summit and reports of injuries and frostbite were growing.

"I have something for you, Lee Chin," Bossman said one day. He showed me a pair of long, flat sticks. In the middle was a strap and the end curved up. "The Norwegian people use these. They are called skis. The mail carriers use them to bring mail across the mountains. Men tell me they can cover forty miles a day with these."

"This is too fine a gift, Bossman. I can't take them."

Bossman threw up his hands. "There is that stubborn Chinese pride. All right, they are mine. But you can use them anytime you want."

"Thank you, Honorable Bossman," I said. "May you be blessed with a hundred sons."

"Whoa, boy. I don't think a hundred sons would be much of a blessing. At any rate, I'm not even married."

I looked at him in surprise. "You do not yet have a wife? Did your parents not find anyone suitable?"

Bossman laughed. "In this country we find our own wives. We court them. Take them for walks, have dinner at their house, go to church with them. Then, if we want to get married, we ask her father's permission. But the girl has already said yes, and talked to her father."

"In my country the parents arrange such matters. My parents will soon be looking for me. They will look for a girl who will be helpful to my mother and yet can work in the fields if needed."

"And in between helping your mother and working in the fields, she is supposed to give you lots of sons, too? Whoo-eee, boy. Are you picking a wife or buying a mule?" Bossman exclaimed.

When I bristled, he shook his head. "I should not have said that. Who knows? Maybe arranged marriages do work better. Don't think it would work for American women, though," he lowered his voice. "Do you know some of them want the right to vote?"

"I do not know this word," I said.

"Every four years, every man gets to help pick a new president," Bossman explained. "But of course women are too emotional to make decisions like that. Heck, they might pick a man just because he's handsome. Women don't really understand politics."

I marveled at this. What an amazing country this was that even an ordinary man could pick the rulers. In China, a dynasty might last for hundreds of years.

Bossman promised to teach me more about voting later. He helped me strap on the skis and watched as I practiced. At first I was awkward, but I quickly learned how to guide my way with the poles.

"Jumping Jehoshaphat!" he exclaimed after watching for a few minutes. "You take to those skis like you was a Norwegian instead of Chinese."

I used the skis every chance I had. They made walking in deep snow easier and they were fun. I was impatient for our day off so I could try them out somewhere away from camp. I got up early on Sunday to discover that it had snowed all night, and now there was at least another foot of fresh snow.

Zhang Wei gave me a bowl of cold rice and some tea. "Be careful," he warned. "You are not used to the snow. There are avalanches in the mountains. I heard a whole camp near the summit was swept away."

"Thank you for your warning, Honorable Uncle. I will be careful," I said.

"Good," he said. "I have grown quite fond of you, and I do not want to have to train another to take your place."

I set off through the woods, moving slowly and trying to balance with the poles. I found a few places where

I could slide down several feet. It was an exhilarating feeling that would have been even better if I had someone to share it with. I thought of Yi and a heavy feeling of sadness nearly took my breath away.

There was a hillside in front of me. It was not too steep and almost bare of trees and bush. I tried to scrape up enough courage to slide all the way down the big hill. Suddenly, there was a swoosh of snow as someone else on skis stopped beside me.

"I didn't know you China boys knew how to ski," said the curly-haired son of Mr. McGee.

"I am just learning," I said.

"Are you going down that hill?" he asked.

I wished this boy would leave. "I am considering it."

"Scared?" he taunted.

"Watch me," he said when I did not answer. "You can push yourself off with the poles. Watch how I move my body. You can slow yourself down with the poles, too." With a spray of snow, he was off, gliding gracefully down the hill. "Now you," he shouted.

I did not want to try with this boy watching me, but I did not want to listen to the taunts I would hear if I did not. Taking a deep breath, I pushed myself off with the poles. At first it was good, and I was flying faster and faster down the hill. Then my legs began separating with one ski going one way and the other moving in another direction.

"Slow yourself down," the boy shouted.

I tried to stop myself by jamming the poles down hard; unfortunately, the poles and my arms stopped, but my body kept moving forward. Suddenly, I was somersaulting, tumbling over and over in the wet, cold snow.

"Are you all right?" I saw his worried face above me.

"I am not hurt," I said, trying to stand.

He gave me a hand to help and then burst into loud laughter. "That was the funniest thing I ever saw."

I was humiliated and angry. "Do you Americans know it is not polite to laugh at another's misfortune?"

He nodded, overcome with a new burst of laughter. "I know. I'm sorry. But it really was funny. I fell like that when I was learning and now I know why everyone laughed at me."

I shook the snow off my clothes. "I guess it did look funny."

It was starting to snow again—big flakes that quickly covered our tracks. "We had better head back," I said, growing nervous. "The snow will cover our tracks."

"I know the way back," he boasted.

The snow was so thick I could hardly see him. "I still think we should start back," I repeated.

"I suppose you're right. We can't see to ski, anyway." He picked up his poles and we started up the hill.

"My name is Sam," he said. Before I could respond, he said, "I know your name. Lee Chin. That's all my father talks about. I heard him talking to my mother. 'Lee Chin learns so quickly. Lee Chin has an artist's eye.'"

"I am only a kitchen boy. Your father's words are far too kind."

"My father wishes I was interested in taking pictures," Sam said.

"Your father understands that you are interested in surveying," I said. "He is proud of you."

Sam stopped and looked at me. "Do you think so?"

Before I could answer, he held up his hand. "Do you hear something?"

I heard a muffled rumble and looked up at the craggy peak above us. Through the thick curtain of falling snow, I saw a crack appear, and the whole side of the mountain seemed to move. Before I truly understood what I was seeing, Sam grabbed my arm.

"Avalanche!" he screamed, just as I was struck with a wall of snow. Over and over I tumbled, violently pushed along by the heavy snow. Then, suddenly, I stopped.

It was utterly silent and I had no idea which way was up. My hand had made a small pocket of air over my face, but I knew that would not last long. I thought of the men at camp talking about the workers who had disappeared in an avalanche near the summit tunnel. They said some of their

bodies would not be found until spring. Was that to be my fate also?

No! I squirmed frantically. I could feel that I still had one ski, although the other one seemed to be lost. By wiggling, I managed to reach the ski and tug it loose. Holding it, I poked in the direction I hoped was up. I saw bright flashes in my eyes and knew that I was running out of air. A desperate sob caught in my throat, and I stabbed the ski again.

There was a breath of air. Gasping, I moved the ski back and forth, using it to dig myself free. "Sam," I called. "Where are you?"

We had been standing right next to each other when the avalanche hit, so he should be close by. The thick snow made it nearly impossible to see, but suddenly I spied a pole jutting out of the snow. I ran to the spot and started digging frantically. I found his foot and pulled with all my might. I finally freed his face, but it was pinched and silent, with no sign of life.

"No!" I shouted. "You can't be dead." With my fist I hit his chest in anger, tears welling in my eyes.

Sam's body seemed to jerk and he made a rasping, choking sound as he sucked in the life-giving air. His eyes flew open. "Are you crying for me, Lee Chin?" he said, with a weak grin.

I brushed at my eyes. "The snow made my eyes weep."

Sam struggled to sit up. "It's almost dusk. You had better try getting back to camp. I don't think I can make it." He pulled up his pants leg to show me his leg that was dark purple and swelling rapidly.

I took a deep breath. It was plain that Sam could not make it back to camp. I wasn't even sure I could make it in the dark, let alone bring others back to this spot. "My honorable uncle broke his leg once. They put sticks on it so he could not move the broken bone," I said.

"The ski," Sam said. "If you could break it somehow."

I picked up the ski and, using all my strength, put my foot across it so it bent in half. The ski broke with a loud crack. After I bent it back and forth several times, the two ends came apart. "We need something to tie it on."

Sam fumbled in his pocket and pulled out a round ball of cloth. "Dry socks," he crowed.

I grinned at him. I knew from the pinched look around his eyes that he was in a lot of pain. Yet he remained cheerful. I took off his shoe and the sock he was wearing. I took two socks and tied them firmly so they were holding the boards in place. Then I put one of the clean, dry socks back on his foot.

It was still snowing. I looked around for anything I could use to make a shelter. . . .

"In school we learned about people in the far north who make houses out of snow," Sam said.

"How do they stay warm?" I asked.

"I guess it's warm inside. 'Course, they probably had furs on the floor."

I was doubtful, thinking of the few minutes I had struggled, buried in the snow.

"It will work," Sam insisted. "You dig a little tunnel going in." He looked around and, for the first time, I saw fear in his eyes. "There might be wolves out here. Or bears."

At the bottom of the hill where we had skied, the snow from the avalanche was piled high. There were several pine trees buried so deep that only the tops were exposed. I started tunneling in the space between two trees. The snow was heavy and wet, and I patted the ceiling and sides, hoping it would not cave in. Then I scooped out a small space, pushing the snow ahead of me through the tunnel. Finally, I broke off boughs of fragrant pine needles to lay several inches thick on the floor of the snow cave.

I came back to where Sam was still sitting. "I think I can drag you backwards," I said. "You can help push yourself along with your good foot."

I grabbed him under his arms and slowly dragged him to the cave. It was completely dark now and I had to feel around for the entrance.

I crawled in first so I could help Sam pull himself inside. He flopped back on the pine boughs. "This is great. You don't have anything to eat, do you?"

"I did not plan on being gone this long," I answered.

"My leg really hurts. Do you think anyone is looking for us?"

"Maybe for you," I said. "As soon as there is enough light, I will go for help," I promised.

I slept fitfully and I was awake long before the first hint of daylight crept through our tunnel door. Sam was moaning softly as he slept. I crawled past him carefully and wiggled through the tunnel. For a minute I stood there in dismay. The snow and the avalanche made everything look different. What if I became lost?

All of the ski poles were gone. I could make good time on the skis using the poles, but without them I wasn't sure. Finally, I left the skis to mark the snow cave and set off on foot to get help.

I knew I had to go back up the hill. I was afraid to climb near the avalanche snow, for fear it would slide. I circled around the hill, slogging through snow nearly up to my waist in places. Finally, I found a wooded area where I could pull myself up tree by tree. At the top I paused, trying to mentally retrace my steps of the day before. The snow had covered every trace of my tracks, but I set off the way I hoped was right. Then, suddenly, I thought I heard something. I stopped, my breath ragged from exertion, and listened. There it was again. A voice, calling, but too far

away to be heard distinctly. I plunged through the snow, heading for the voice.

"Help!" I yelled, but my voice seemed to disappear into the vast wilderness. I listened again, but the voice was gone.

"Help!" I screamed again. Then, suddenly, not very far away, I heard: "Sam? Lee Chin?"

"We're here," I called. In just a few minutes, I was surrounded by friends: Mr. McGee, Bossman, Zhang Wei, and several men from my crew. Two men were dispatched to make some kind of stretcher, and I led the others back down the hill.

"Jumping Jehoshaphat, boy. I thought you were done for. Did you make this shelter?" Bossman asked.

"It is not very good," I said. "But it was the only thing we could think to do. Sam told me about people who live in snow houses."

Mr. McGee and Bossman carried Sam out of the snow shelter. "That was a great shelter," Mr. McGee said, overhearing our conversation. "Sam tells me you saved his life."

"I did little," I said. "Perhaps the mountain god does not want boys with curly red hair."

"I guess he didn't want someone with a girly pigtail, either," Sam teased, as they lifted him onto the stretcher.

chapter eleven

New Year

Chinese people believe that it is a virtue to be humble. It was very difficult to remain that way with Bossman and Mr. McGee telling everyone that I was a hero and saying that I saved Sam's life. Even Mr. Strobridge stopped by to thank me.

Mr. McGee took Sam back to Sacramento, and after a few days, things settled back to normal. Tunnels one and two were done, the track laid, and, in December, trains ran from the town of Cisco ninety-two miles to Sacramento. Huang Chow said the bosses still were not happy because the Union Pacific had finished nearly three hundred miles of track.

The American workers had a holiday in December. They called it Christmas, and Bossman explained they were celebrating the birth of the one god's son, Jesus. He told me about some kings traveling to see the baby and bringing presents. It was an interesting story.

 The Iron Dragon

Bossman gave me an orange. "On this day we give each other presents."

"But I don't have any present for you," I protested.

Bossman sighed. "Just say thank you, Lee Chin."

I grinned at him. "Thank you."

Snow fell nearly every day and some of the crews were sent back to Sacramento until the weather cleared. The snow was so heavy that many days the trains could not get through even when they brought in giant snowplows. Rumors said that they were going to build sheds over the worst places. Our crew was being sent to the summit tunnel, but we had to wait weeks for a change in the weather so we could move our camp.

As soon as the Iron Dragon made it through with supplies, we loaded wagons and carts, and began the trek to the new campground near the summit tunnel. I could see the engine Missouri Bill had hauled up the mountain. The summit tunnel was long. Mr. Strobridge had crews working both ends, but when even that proved too slow, he had ordered the workers to dig a shaft in the center. The stripped-down locomotive was used to haul up the rocks and debris. When the bottom was reached, workers would be able to blast their way through until they met the teams coming from the ends of the tunnel.

Zhang Wei was thrilled with his new cookhouse. It had real tables and chairs and an iron wood-burning cookstove

104

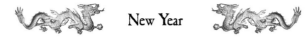

with a baking box. He rubbed his hands together in delight. "We can have roast duck for our New Year feast."

I gulped. Zhang Wei had a pen of chickens and he occasionally killed one for a special dinner. Chickens were silly, bad-tempered birds, not to my liking, and it did not bother me to find one dropped in the cooking pot. I liked the ducks, however. It had been my job to care for the ducks. They had arrived on one of the supply trains and moved with us to the new camp. I had fed them well. Now they were plump and fat.

Zhang Wei gave me a sideways glance. "I told you not to name them."

I went out to the cages and scattered some feed. "I have some bad news," I told them. The smallest duck, which I had named Min, meaning "clever," stuck his bill through the cage and nibbled at my hand. Min was my favorite. "Maybe it's best you don't know what is coming. At any rate, it is still a month until the New Year."

The Americans had already had their New Year, and for them, it didn't seem to be much of a holiday. Our Chinese calendar was different. Our celebration would start on the first day of the first lunar month and last about fifteen days.

The day before the New Year celebration began at home, my mother would carefully sweep and dust every corner of the house to get rid of any lingering bad luck. Then she would hide the broom and dustpan so that good luck could

not get lost. This was the day she would burn the paper kitchen god after putting honey on his mouth so that he would say only good things to the Jade Emperor who rules the other side. My father would pay any debts he owed, and, on good years, everyone got new clothes and haircuts, and lucky signs were hung about the house.

Every day of the fifteen-day celebration had a special tradition. For example, on the second day, everyone was kind to dogs since this was their birthday. People had their birthday on the seventh day, and parents, aunts, uncles, and grandparents gave the children gifts of money wrapped in red paper for good luck.

I explained these customs to Bossman. "You Celestials do have some good ideas," he said. "I don't know about the kitchen god and all that, but cleaning house, settling debts, and making a new start every year sounds like a good idea."

"We have several feast days during the celebration," I told him. "Zhang Wei will make dumplings and a special cake to celebrate."

"I would really like to taste your food sometime," Bossman said.

"I will ask Zhang Wei if I can bring you some," I said.

Zhang Wei gave his permission when I asked. He changed his mind about Bossman after Sam and I had been lost in the avalanche.

"He was genuinely concerned for you," Zhang Wei had told me afterward. "His help during the mudslide was not unnoticed. I believe he may be an honorable man."

I looked in the pot and dished out rice, vegetables, and chicken. I carefully removed the chicken's head and feet, knowing that would not be pleasing to American tastes. Zhang Wei put a dumpling, pan-fried on one side and steamed on the other, into another bowl.

"Unless he is an unusual American, he won't like this," he said. "I have heard that they eat nothing but potatoes and beans with cow meat. And," he added with a shudder of distaste, "they drink milk from those cows."

Bossman sniffed at the bowl. "It smells very good," he admitted. He tasted the food cautiously and then with gusto. "This is delicious," he said when the plate was empty. "Tell Zhang Wei he is an amazing cook."

"He will be pleased to hear that you liked it," I said.

"It is too bad more of my countrymen don't know how good your food is. Zhang Wei could open a restaurant and become a rich man."

Right after the start of our New Year, it began to snow one day and didn't stop for the next four days. Everyone had to take a turn shoveling, but even so, we could hardly keep up. Snow had to be shoveled off the rooftops. The blacksmith shop was so buried that we had to make steps

going down to the doorway. Still, the workers at the tunnel kept on, although progress was slow.

On my birthday, Zhang Wei gave me some money wrapped in red paper, and so did Bossman, who remembered what I had told him about our traditions. Huang Chow gave me several strings of firecrackers he had ordered in a shipment from San Francisco. But there was little time to enjoy them. I had hoped to see my father, but he did not come to visit.

There was now more than twenty feet of snow on the ground, and men worked around the clock, digging snow tunnels between buildings and to the tunnels. Several crews were swept away by avalanches and some workers disappeared. I thought back to the first time I saw snow and how I thought it was beautiful. Still, there was a strange beauty to it. Even though there were hundreds of men at the summit, the snow muffled the sound.

On the rare occasions when the snow stopped falling, you could see the stars at night, almost close enough to touch. The lanterns lighting the tunnel entrance cast a glow around the summit, illuminating the engine, now called the Blue Goose. It hunched over the mountain like a true Iron Dragon, gobbling up rocks and spitting them out.

Almost every day a wagon of injured workers, some hit by flying rock from explosions and some with frostbitten feet and hands, was sent back to Cisco. From there, they

went to Sacramento. Most of the men did not trust American doctors, but in Sacramento and San Francisco, there were Chinese herb doctors to treat them. Some came back when they had been cured, but most we never saw again.

The bitter cold continued. I traveled between the cook camps inside a tunnel dug into the snow. Small windows were cut in the ceiling to give light. Often the supply trains could not get through and food supplies were short. Some supplies were brought in on the road, which was at a lower altitude. From there, supplies were brought to the summit by sled. One of the supply sleds brought me two letters one day.

"Two letters," several of the men teased me. "Who knew our little Lee Chin was so important."

Blushing, I hid the letters away in my sleeping mat until I could find someone to help me read them. With Bossman's help, I was learning to write English, but I still could not read Chinese. The first letter was from my mother. I had not heard from her since I had sent her the picture. After my evening chores were done, I took it to Wu Chang, my old teacher.

"To my son in the land of Gold Mountain," the letter began. Wu Chang read:

> *It has been a long time, I know, but it was difficult for your elder brother to go to the city and find a letter writer. With the*

money you and your honorable father have sent, your brothers have been able to raise a good crop this year and even buy a new ox and some chickens. Elder Brother has put away seeds for next year and still has managed to save a few coins. He is planning on buying another small piece of land. He wishes to marry soon and says that we need more land to feed a wife and children for himself and Middle Brother.

Elder Brother went to the rich man's house to see about buying some land. He saw Sunshine carrying heavy buckets of water for the master's bath. She could not talk, she said, because the head cook beats her if she works too slow. Poor little Sunshine. I hope that they find a husband for her when she is older and that she doesn't become a concubine to the master.

I showed your picture to all the uncles, cousins, and aunts, and we are all amazed at how much the likeness looks like you. I put it on the shelf next to the ancestor shrine. It will keep you in my mind until I see you again.

An anger burned in me so deep that I scarcely heard the end of the letter. How could my father be so cruel? The rich man was very old and he already had four young concubines. Sunshine could become another young girl who would belong to the rich man without the honor of marriage.

With a heavy heart, I took the second letter to Bossman. He had been teaching me to read English, but I still needed help. Sam wrote that his foot was healing and he was walking with something he called crutches. He was back in school and could hardly wait until summer, when his father promised that he would try to find me again. The letter was signed, "Your friend, Sam."

I liked the way that sounded. I had never had a real friend before. There were my brothers and Yi, but they were family. I folded the letters and tucked them under my sleeping mat.

In spite of the fact that Mr. Strobridge and Mr. Crocker had said they would not use nitroglycerin again, they were so frustrated with the slow progress that they gave orders for it to be used on the tunnel.

Huang Chow was not happy, but, as usual, he said nothing, only bowing politely and passing the news on to the men. "They will bring the ingredients up separately and mix only what is needed," he told the men.

The man who mixed the nitro was a Scottish chemist named James Howden. Each day, he mixed up only what was needed of the yellow, oily liquid. After what had happed to Yi and the others, the explosives experts were very careful. At dinner the men talked of how much faster the work was going.

At last, it was the fifteenth day and time for the final New Year feast. Zhang Wei took care of the ducks when I was working with Bossman. Zhang Wei had been pleased that Bossman had enjoyed the food, and to my surprise, he suggested I invite Bossman to the feast. I told myself that I would never be able to eat the ducks, but the smell of the crackling brown skin roasting made my mouth water. Bossman wanted to bring something but agonized over what he could bring that the men would like. He finally decided on cornmeal biscuits because he knew that I liked them.

Zhang Wei had also invited my father. He came and handed me several coins wrapped in red paper. "I missed your birthday celebration," he said.

I bowed. "Thank you for remembering me," I said. I had not seen my father since the argument about Sunshine. He filled his plate with Zhang Wei's good cooking and sat beside me.

"My crew is being sent back to build snow sheds over the track where the drifting was the worst this winter," he said. "I will not be able to see you for awhile."

"I have been offered a job if I stay in this country when the railroad is finished," I said.

My father stared at me. "It was a mistake to bring you, Chin. You are too easily influenced by the barbarians. When the job is done, you will return home. Your brothers have followed my instructions and purchased more land. You will have to assume your share of the work." My father had little more to say to me.

The men were surprised to see the big red-haired giant at their table. They ate in nervous silence, watching from the corners of their eyes. But Bossman had promised that this time he would try to eat with chopsticks, and the results were so disastrous that the whole room was soon laughing, cheering when Bossman managed to get a bit of food into his mouth and offering demonstrations when he did not.

My father watched all this with a frown. "The red-haired one does not belong at the New Year feast," he said.

"Do not come to me with any more of your foolish ideas," my father said to me. "When we are done, you will return home with me!" He quickly finished his meal and left to go back to his camp.

Someone finally tried the cornmeal muffins and pronounced them good. I could see that Bossman was pleased as the plate was emptied. Even though they did not speak each other's language, Zhang Wei and Bossman

managed to communicate with signs and some translating from me.

"Zhang Wei would like to learn how to make these muffins," I told Bossman.

"Tell him to come to the cookhouse, and I will show him," Bossman said. "But in return he must show me how to make these dumplings."

chapter twelve

Strike

"Union Pacific sent some spies into town," Bossman told me one day. "Mr. Crocker and his brother are pretending that they believe the men are writing a book about the Central Pacific. They're telling the men that it may be another two years before we get through the summit."

"I heard we were almost through," I said.

"Exactly," Bossman said. "But if the men tell the leaders of the Union Pacific that we're way behind, they may not be in such a hurry."

"We should have spies, too," I said.

Bossman laughed. "We do."

"I hope they are not being tricked like we are doing to their men," I said.

Bossman nodded. "So far I don't think they have been discovered. The Union Pacific is far ahead of us. Until now they've been building on fairly flat land, but they have the

Rocky Mountains ahead of them. After we pass Truckee we'll be in flat, easy country. Crocker is bragging that his men can lay ten miles of track in one day. I hope no one calls him on that, because it's impossible."

A few weeks later I heard a rumor that many men on the other side of Truckee were quitting the Central Pacific and taking jobs offered in mines, sawmills, and farms. There were enough desertions that Crocker and Strobridge were worried they would not have enough men left to finish the job. They planned to bring more workers from China. Zhang Wei said that he heard some of the foremen were harshly treating the men who were trying to leave.

Perhaps the desertions were the reason Mr. Crocker raised the wages to thirty-five dollars a month. Some of the men were pleased when Huang Chow told them, but others were not. "It should be forty dollars. We have to pay our own board and they even take the cost of our shovels and carts out of our pay," one of the men complained.

The grumbling might have continued, but a new foreman was assigned to our crew. We knew the minute we saw him that he was going to be trouble. I was pouring the tea into the kegs when he suddenly appeared.

"You yellow slant-eyes will take your break when I say," he shouted, although none of the men could understand him. He raised his whip and cracked it over the head of one of the workers, who jumped back in alarm.

Huang Chow hurried forward. "I am Huang Chow, the headman," he said, bowing politely.

"I haven't got time to bother with your peculiar names," the new foreman said. "You will come when I call John Chinaman, understood?"

Huang Chow nodded. "There is no need to use your whip. These men are all hard workers and they are free men, not slaves."

"Maybe you would like to feel my whip?" the foreman sneered. He stood close to Huang Chow, towering over him, and spat on the dirty snow. "You tell your men they take their break when I say and they quit work when I say."

Huang Chow nodded. He turned without his usual polite bow and relayed the foreman's message. The men listened quietly, their faces unreadable.

That night the men were nearly two hours late getting back to camp. An angry buzz spread through the camp.

"It is time to strike," muttered some of the younger men. "We should have done it long ago, when Wu Ling wanted to strike."

"That is not our way," Huang Chow protested.

"We are in America, so we must use their ways to make them understand," someone shouted.

"The Americans are too strong. They will punish us," others argued. "They will find other workers and we will be sent home."

I listened carefully, not sure which side was right. Our wages were better than we would receive at home. Still, while we did most of the work, the Americans held all the good jobs and made better wages.

The men, especially the young ones, argued back and forth, and runners were sent to the other camps. During the next few weeks, men came from the other camps, even as far away as Truckee, on the other side of the summit, to plan a strike.

"Save your money," the strike leaders admonished. "We will have to buy our food and supplies during the strike."

The strike started on Monday. All along the track and tunnels men did not report for work. I wondered what Bossman thought when I did not report for work. That afternoon Mr. Strobridge galloped into camp at noon and demanded to see Huang Chow. "What is this? Why are your men not working?"

"The men have some demands before they will return to work," Huang Chow said unhappily. "They want forty dollars a month, ten hour workdays, and eight-hour days in the tunnels."

Mr. Strobridge's face turned red with anger. "I make the rules, not you."

After he galloped away, the men were silent. For the next two days, everyone stayed in their camps, quietly washing clothes, cleaning up the sleeping quarters, and

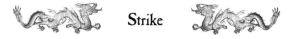

talking in small groups. On the second day of the strike, Mr. Strobridge's personal servant came to camp to announce that no more deliveries of food and supplies would be allowed through. "He says if you do not return to work by Monday, you will not be paid for June."

Although nothing was said, everyone knew the strike had been broken. The men were prepared to buy food for a time, but there was no food to buy, and there was no way to arrange delivery of food for thousands of men. The next Monday, everyone went back to work. The foreman had been replaced, but nothing else changed.

Bossman met me at the door on Monday morning. "Well, so you've decided to come back to work," he said in his booming voice.

"I beg your forgiveness, Bossman. I had to stay with my countrymen," I said.

"You don't owe me an apology. I understood. I don't suppose Crocker and Strobridge did though. I expect they were plenty surprised that your people would rebel at all."

I picked up the water kegs and headed for the door.

"If the Irish had been on strike, there would have been riots and fights. You Chinese are orderly even when you strike," Bossman remarked.

"That is our way," I said.

"You'll need a little fight in you to make it in this country," Bossman said.

"As soon as this job is finished, I will go home and help my father and brothers farm," I said.

Bossman shook his head. "Jumping Jehoshaphat! That would be a terrible waste, Lee Chin. You are a good artist, you speak pretty good English, and you're learning to read, write, and do sums. You're a quick learner. Do you really think you would be happy always being the third brother on a farm?"

I did not answer. I had been trying to swallow such feelings for months. I was tempted by Mr. McGee's offer, but my duty was to return home. I did miss my mother and brothers, but at home I would be forced to see Sunshine living in slavery. I thought I had enough money saved to buy her freedom, but if my father would not take her back, where could she go?

It was August when the workers finally broke through in the summit tunnel. It was only a small hole, and months of work still remained—enlarging the opening and carrying away tons of debris, before the track could be laid. Still, the mountain had been pierced—a feat that people had said could not be done. Four hundred men had toiled twenty-four hours a day for more than a year. They had worked through the brutal cold, and in snow so deep they had to dig snow tunnels to travel back and forth. The tunnel was so well engineered that when the workers broke through, they were only a couple of inches off.

Bossman told me the tunnel was 1,659 feet long. There was a huge celebration in the camps with firecrackers and we had the rest of the day off. Some of the men were sent down the mountain to start making grade into Nevada, but our gang would stay here until the tunnel was opened. Even though it was summer, at this high altitude there was still snow on the ground and ice covered the tunnel headings. But everyone fell to their jobs with renewed vigor.

The months passed, including a brief few weeks of warmer weather, and then it was winter again.

Another New Year came and passed, and I was now fourteen. I had not seen my father in six months. Just after the New Year, I received another letter from my mother. She told me that she saw Sunshine during the New Year celebration and had been allowed to give her some cake.

"My heart ached to see her," my mother wrote. "I do not think they are kind to her in that house. She looks frail and sad."

I reflected on that letter for weeks after it came. The problem grew like a dragon in my mind. I could scarcely think of anything else. But I could not find a solution.

Mr. McGee and Sam had come twice. Each time, Mr. McGee had taught me more about the camera, and I could now make up the chemicals to develop the pictures without supervision. Mr. McGee looked through my drawings. He liked a picture I had made of Bossman, and another of the

Iron Dragon crossing a bridge. The last one he chose was a picture of Mr. Strobridge taking his children for a boat ride on Donner Lake. The children were dressed in their brightly colored clothes. The girls had their hair in curls with bows and white straw hats to shield their faces from the sun. The girls giggled and squealed as their father splashed them with water.

"I will frame them and put them in my shop," Mr. McGee said. "Maybe someone will buy them." He looked thoughtfully at the picture of Mr. Strobridge. "I believe I will show this one to Mr. Strobridge. It is really a lovely picture."

One day, not long after that, I sat with Bossman, struggling to read *Treasure Island*. It was a gift from Sam and it was an exciting story, but my mind wandered. Finally, Bossman closed the book. "What troubles you, Chin?"

I decided to tell Bossman about Sunshine, and how seeing Mr. Strobridge with his daughters and hearing their joyful laughter made me feel sad.

"Jumping Jehoshaphat!" Bossman exclaimed loudly. "What a terrible burden for a boy."

Bossman scratched at his wild red beard while he thought. "You must go to Zhang Wei. Maybe there is a way to bring her to this country."

"How would I care for her?" I asked, shaking my head.

"We'll figure that out later," Bossman said. "Maybe your friend Mr. McGee can help. He seems like a good and thoughtful person. The important thing right now is to get her out of slavery. I know Zhang Wei will help you."

Zhang Wei and Bossman had become friends over the past months. It was a strange friendship since neither one knew more than a few words of the other's language. Still, Bossman had managed to teach Zhang Wei a card game he called poker. Instead of playing for money, they gambled with pebbles, which the winner kept in a jar and used to taunt the other.

I approached Zhang Wei that evening. "What are you going to do when the job is done?" I asked Zhang Wei as we worked together.

Zhang Wei shook his head. "I have been thinking on this. With my wife gone, there is nothing to return to at home. Maybe I will stay in this country."

I looked at him, surprised by his response. I had not known he was thinking this way.

"Maybe I could go to Sacramento and try to open a restaurant. There are quite a few Chinese there."

"Bossman says that if more Americans would taste our food, they would buy it," I said.

"I think it will take a long time for that to happen. I will be in the land of the Jade Emperor long before that."

I took a deep breath. "Honorable Uncle, I have been thinking on something for a long time. Perhaps you could help me?"

Zhang Wei must have seen my troubled look, because he poured us each some tea and told me to sit at one of the wooden tables. Slowly, I told him everything—how my father had sold Sunshine and how I worried that she would be sold again. "I think I have saved enough to buy her freedom and pay for her passage here."

Zhang Wei was silent for a few minutes. "And then what, Lee Chin? How would you take care of her?"

"I too am thinking about staying here," I answered. "Mr. McGee said if I stay, he will give me a job."

"What do you know of raising a girl?" Zhang Wei asked. "You are still a boy yourself."

"If I wait until I am grown, it may be too late for her," I said.

Zhang Wei stood up. "I will think about your problem. I could write to the agent of the Six Companies and they could arrange her passage. But we must decide what to do when she is here."

"Maybe she could dress as a boy and help you," I suggested.

"We will have to take Wu Chang into our confidence. I will ask him to write a letter and see if it is possible,"

Zhang Wei said. He hesitated. "Your father will not forgive such defiance."

"I know," I said. "I have thought much on this problem. I cannot bear the thought of Sunshine living as a slave." I bowed low. "I know I will be disobeying my father's commands, but I must do what I believe is right. Thank you for your help, Honorable Uncle."

"Your father is a foolish man," Zhang Wei said. "I would have been proud to call you a son, Lee Chin."

chapter thirteen

Waiting for Sunshine

Wu Chang wrote the letter and it was sent on the next train going to Sacramento. In addition to paying the cost to buy my sister, Zhang Wei suggested I enclose some money for the agent—a bribe—for all his trouble. A few weeks later, we had an answer. The agent was making the trip home to sign up more workers. He would bring her back with him if he could find her. Now there was nothing to do but wait.

When Mr. Strobridge galloped in with our pay a few nights later, he said to Huang Chow, "Where is the one called Lee Chin?"

"He is busy with chores," Huang Chow answered. "Has he done something wrong?"

"Go get him," Mr. Strobridge ordered.

Huang Chow hurried to fetch me from the cookhouse, where I had just finished sweeping. "What have you done?" he hissed. "I told you not to draw attention to yourself."

I felt a rising panic. Had Mr. Strobridge found out about the letter and the plan to disguise Sunshine as a boy? With great trepidation, I walked out to see Mr. Strobridge, still mounted on his horse.

"You are Lee Chin?" Mr. Strobridge asked. He looked surprised. "I remember you. You are the one who knew all the body parts."

I bowed. "My English is much better now. Did I do something wrong?"

Mr. Strobridge reached into his saddlebag and pulled out a pouch. He tossed it to me. I could feel that it was heavy with coins when I caught it.

"I do not understand. What is this for?" I said, speaking in the blunt manner of the Americans.

"The picture of my family, boy. . . . McGee said forty dollars was a fair price."

I bowed happily. "You are too kind to this humble artist," I said. I felt the weight of the coins. *Forty dollars!* More than a month's pay! Now I would be certain to have enough money for Sunshine.

"It was a fine picture. Mrs. Strobridge loved it. She is going to hang it in the parlor," he said.

Huang Chow did not speak when Mr. Strobridge had ridden away, but I saw a new respect in his eyes. The other men clamored around me. Not speaking English, they were not sure what had happened. I had to repeat the story for

Zhang Wei and again for Bossman, who pounded me on the back.

"Congratulations, Chin. You're on the way to becoming famous." Then he laughed. "But while you're waiting, you need to go fetch me some water."

The summit tunnel had been finished in November, but there was still a seven-mile gap between Cisco and the summit, and another from the summit down to Truckee. Finally, in June, it was finished and the Central Pacific now had 167 miles of continuous track. We were already packing to go to a new camp in Nevada when a train full of important people made the trip through the summit and on to a new town called Reno.

The special train had one boxcar full of freight, another with luggage and U.S. mail, and three passenger cars. The locomotive was named the Antelope and it was a beautiful sight. The cab was walnut and the wheels were bright red. The brass work was shiny and an antelope had been painted on the headlight. Everyone stopped work to watch it chug up the grade to the summit tunnel, over seven thousand feet high. The American workers cheered, and my people waved their hats and cheered right along with them.

Some crews had been grading the last few months and were nearly three hundred miles ahead of the end of the track. There were nearly three thousand of us, along with four hundred horse-drawn carts heading for a place called

Palisade Canyon. It was in Nevada, near the Humboldt River, Bossman told me.

"What if the agent comes and he cannot find us?" I fretted to Zhang Wei.

"He will find us. Huang Chow sends pay records every week. Have you forgotten, impatient one?" Zhang Wei teased.

I did not like the new camp. It was hot and dry, with few trees, and I missed the mountains—although I did not care if I ever saw snow again. Mr. Crocker had buildings already constructed, and there were platforms so that the tents had a wooden floor for us. For the buildings, he brought in lumber from the sawmills at Truckee. But food, grain for the mules, and water, had to be brought from great distances by wagon.

"Crocker wants your people to take fewer baths or use less water," Bossman told me.

"I will tell Huang Chow," I said. "But the men will not be happy."

When I carried the tea that afternoon, one of the men gave me some news. "We will soon be in the Great Desert. There are snakes there that can swallow a man whole. The Indians are twenty-five feet tall and they eat people."

I nearly dropped my pole. "Where did you hear that?"

"It's true," the man insisted. "Many people are leaving before we get there. I am going. I didn't survive the

freezing snow and blasting with nitroglycerin just to be eaten by an Indian or a snake."

"We have seen a few Indians," I reminded him. "They look just like other people. They are no taller than the Americans."

"These are a tribe of the desert," he insisted. He finished his tea. "You had better go before we get to the desert."

When I got back to camp, I saw a truly amazing sight. There was a train at the end of the track. The first few cars were luxurious, obviously offices and quarters for the railroad. Behind them were several more cars, some nearly four stories high. At the end there were two flatcars with huge water tanks. I saw Bossman carrying supplies to one of the cars. He waved when he saw me.

"Mr. Crocker's idea," he said, pointing to one of the four-story cars. "The bottom is the cooking area, and upstairs are sleeping quarters. He's going to keep this train at the end of the track."

I hurried back to my job with Zhang Wei. As I entered the cookhouse, I saw an important-looking man dressed in a silk jacket. Perched on a crate beside him was a child. She was taller and thinner and dressed as a boy, but there was no mistaking her smile. It was Sunshine.

I hugged her and swung her around while she giggled in delight. "Sunshine! I have waited so long to see you."

"Is it really you, Elder Brother?" she said, wrapping her arms around me and holding tight.

A disapproving sniff from the agent reminded me of my manners. I bowed deeply. "You have found my sister. I am grateful."

"It has been a difficult journey," the agent exclaimed. "I had to hire a driver and pay for a wagon. I will have to add to the cost."

I bowed again. "What do I owe you, Honorable Sir?"

"Three hundred American dollars," he replied.

I heard Zhang Wei gasp, but I nodded. I had just counted the savings in my can hidden by the kitchen god.

"I have two hundred and eighty dollars. Will that do?"

He sniffed into an embroidered handkerchief. "I have endured much hardship."

Zhang Wei spoke. "I have the rest of the money, Lee Chin. You can pay me later."

And so it was done. And now I had a family.

chapter fourteen

Ten Miles in a Day

I had a million questions for Sunshine, but Zhang Wei touched my arm. "The child is exhausted and frightened. Let her rest and you can talk later," he said. He handed her a small bowl of rice and vegetables. "Eat, little one. When you are done there is a sleeping mat for you in the corner."

For the first time, I saw the blue shadows under her eyes. "Honorable Uncle is right," I said. "Sleep and we will talk later."

She stood up to bow, but I shook my head. "You do not need to bow to me."

Sunshine ate only a few bites of food before I saw her eyes closing. Zhang Wei grabbed the bowl before she could drop it, and I picked her up and laid her on the sleeping mat. I could feel the thinness of her body. It seemed as though she weighed almost nothing. Her hair tumbled out of the hat she wore.

"We will have to braid her hair. But if she wears the hat, perhaps we will not have to shave the front," Zhang Wei whispered.

Sunshine slept through the men returning from work and the serving of dinner. She was still sleeping when I headed for the strange new cookhouse on the train. Zhang Wei assured me that she would be safe while I was gone.

"She is here," I exclaimed happily to Bossman.

"Well, I'll be," he said, shaking his head in wonder. "I didn't really think it would happen."

After telling Bossman the good news, he gave me some bad news. "Mr. Strobridge isn't happy today. Nearly one thousand of your countrymen have deserted in the last couple of days. Crocker wants his crew to do at least a mile a day and he's losing all his help."

"I know why," I exclaimed. I quickly told him what the worker had told me about the twenty-five-foot Indians and the giant, man-eating snakes.

Bossman went to the door and pointed down the tracks to one of the nicer train cars. "That's Mr. Crocker's office. You go over there and tell him what you just told me. Go on. He will be happy to know what the problem is."

Timidly, I tapped on the door of Mr. Crocker's office. "I need to talk to Mr. Crocker," I said to the man who opened the door.

The man shook his head. "If you have a problem, go see your headman," he said.

Before I could explain, Mr. Crocker walked up to us. He pointed to his mouth. "We don't speak Chinese," he said loudly. I wondered why when you don't speak their language, people also think you are deaf.

"I speak English well enough. Bossman sent me to tell you something."

Mr. Crocker looked surprised. "You are the painter? Strobridge told me about you. Now what's this you have to tell me?"

When I explained the rumors around the camp, Mr. Crocker laughed. "We had trouble with that before, but nothing this ridiculous. I'll bet the Union Pacific spies have been spreading those rumors to slow us down." He looked thoughtful. "What do you think I should do?"

"Maybe you could take a few men from each camp, maybe the headmen, and take them to the desert so they can come back and tell the men it is not true." I bowed. "Of course, I am only a kitchen boy, so my advice may not be good."

Mr. Crocker gave a hearty laugh. "Your advice is very good."

When my chores were done, Bossman waved me away. "No lessons today. I know you want to get back to your camp."

Sunshine was sitting on a barrel, busy chopping dried mushrooms, when I returned. Zhang Wei had braided her hair and she wore her hat to cover her head.

"Elder Brother. Honorable Uncle has told me I am to be a boy. Now my name is Lee Chang."

She told me her story while we worked. She had been treated badly at the great house. Several of the older girls had been sold to be concubines. One of the married daughters of the great house had taken Sunshine for her personal servant. This woman had not been kind. She gave her only a little to eat and often struck her across the back with a bamboo cane if she was angry.

"You are free now," I told her. "You will never be a slave again. In America, they do not have slaves. They even fought a war to make sure that was so."

The next day, Mr. Crocker did take my advice. Huang Chow was one of the men selected to venture into the desert. "There is no way any human being, let alone someone twenty-five feet high, could live there. The only thing I saw alive were a few sagebrush plants," he reported. Evidently, the other headmen reported the same, because there were no more desertions.

None of the crew seemed to notice that Lee Chang, the new helper, was really a girl. Some men complained about paying wages for another helper, especially one so small.

But when Zhang Wei and I promised to pay her wages, they paid no more attention to her.

I decided to start teaching Sunshine English right away. She liked to help with the chores in the kitchen: washing tables, chopping vegetables, and sweeping the floor. As we worked, I named things, much like Wu Chang had done for me. To my delight, she learned quickly. In only a few weeks, she was speaking well enough to be understood.

Bossman and Zhang Wei cared for her like two old grandfathers, spoiling her with treats and presents. On our birthday at the New Year, I was fifteen and Sunshine turned eleven. For her birthday, Bossman made her a small wooden doll with a smiling painted face and yarn hair. She could only play with it when no one was around, but she loved it. I had Zhang Wei order a small square of silk and some fine needles and thread for her to make the doll an elegant dress.

"She is a princess," Sunshine declared solemnly. Then she sighed. "Her feet are very big for a princess."

"In this country they do not bind girls' feet," I said.

"I am glad," she said. "One of the rich man's daughters had hers done when I was there. They bent her toes back and bound them. Then they made her walk on them until the bones broke. She screamed all day and all night. Then she got a terrible sickness. Her feet and legs turned black, and she died."

In China, very small feet were considered beautiful. For centuries, young girls' feet were bound until they were only a few inches long. Most women with bound feet could hardly walk, so poor women, who were needed to work in the fields, did not have to undergo this torture. Sunshine looked at her feet.

"My feet are getting big," she said. "They told me I would not have my feet bound because I needed to walk to do chores. They said I would have ugly feet."

Zhang Wei had been listening. "My wife had beautiful, big feet."

Sunshine looked very pleased. "Good. My princess will declare everyone in her kingdom must have big, beautiful feet."

In the meantime, we had reached the desert. Huang Chow's report had been true. There was nothing but sand and rocks. There was an unpleasant creature called a scorpion. Mr. Crocker told all the headmen to tell their men to always check their boots before they put them on in the morning, because scorpions sometimes crawled inside them during the night. Several men were stung. Although one man was sick for several days, no one died.

The only thing good about the desert was that it was flat and the track laying went quickly. We were far ahead of the tracklayers, but news of their progress came daily

over the telegraph wires. Bossman said they were doing a mile a day, sometimes more.

For the most part, the grading went quickly, too, although there were a few places to fill. The work went so quickly that we had to move every few days. One day there would be a busy town of five thousand people, and the next day there would only be the remains of a few cooking fires and the town would be ten miles away. Stretching endlessly behind would be the tracks, dotted every few feet with telegraph poles. At night, the last telegraph pole would be connected to one of the railcars that served as Crocker's office. He would send a message down the completed track, ordering supplies for the next day.

For months we had gone through land with no cities or people. Bossman said there were several big towns in a place called Utah. Some people lived there who believed in having several wives, Bossman told me.

"In China a man can have more than one wife, although many do not."

"Jumping Jehoshaphat!" Bossman exclaimed. "What about a wife? For you, someday, I mean. I don't see any Chinese women in this country."

"Zhang Wei is going to send to China for a wife when we are done. The Six Companies will help him arrange it. I can do that, too, when I am older."

Bossman took off his hat and scratched the bald top of his head. "I think I'd rather see them first. What if she's a mean one who is always yelling at you to wipe your feet?"

Sunshine had been quietly sitting in a corner, playing with her doll. Over the past weeks, she had put on weight and her hair and skin had a healthy glow. Best of all, her smile brightened and she was comfortable enough with Bossman to tease him. She jumped up and shook her finger at Bossman. "Look at that dirt on the floor. Haven't I told you to wipe your feet?"

Bossman picked her up and swung her around. "This is what I do to bossy little girls," he said as she giggled and squealed.

Suddenly, we realized someone was standing in the doorway. Bossman quickly put Sunshine down, but it was obviously too late. To my relief, it was Sam.

"Sam," I shouted happily. "I haven't seen you for so long."

"I didn't know there were girls in your camp," Sam said, looking from Bossman to Sunshine.

Then, of course, I had to let one more person in on my secret. "How are you going to take care of her?" he asked. "I have two sisters and they're a real pain. They're always giggling and getting into my stuff."

"Sunshine is not like that," I said.

Sam's leg was healed, although he still walked with a slight limp. "You'll have to tell my father," he said as we walked along the track together, with Sunshine tagging along behind.

"Do you think he won't let me work for him if he knows?"

Sam shook his head. "It's not that. He was going to have you live in our house while you are learning. My mother says that's the least we can do when you saved my life."

I shook my head. "I didn't really save your life."

"I say you did. Anyway, my father wants to see you."

Mr. McGee was taking pictures of the track that had been laid just past our camp. He waved when he saw us.

"Oh, good. Sam found you. I haven't got much time," he said. "There was a snow slide not far from Cisco and a trestle collapsed. Several passenger trains are stranded and my magazine wants me to take some pictures. I wanted to give you this," he said, reaching into his pocket and handing me two twenty-dollar gold pieces. "I sold another of your pictures."

I bowed. "Thank you, Honorable Sir."

"Have you decided if you are going to work for me? I believe another six months and the railroad will be done."

Sunshine had trailed along behind us. With her long braid and hat pulled low, she looked like a young boy.

"There are two of us," I said. I explained the story once again, wondering the whole time if he would rescind his offer. What would I do then? I could not return to China.

Mr. McGee stared at Sunshine. He knelt down and smiled gently. "Hello, child."

My sister bowed low. Then she stood up and very clearly said, "My name is Sunshine."

The whistle of the train rang out from down the track. "We need to go," Mr. McGee said urgently as he gathered up his things. "I will be back soon. We will talk then."

Sam waved good-bye as he ran after his father.

I stared after them with emptiness in the pit of my stomach. Was that the last I would see of them? And what would I do if Mr. McGee decided Sunshine and I were too much trouble? Sunshine was staring at me, but I smiled and took her hand, pretending nothing was wrong.

Mr. McGee and Sam did not come back soon, though I watched for them every day. The weather had turned very cold, below zero day after day. Bossman explained that although we were still in desert country, we were very high—nearly as high as Cisco. The work still went on, although the graders could not use their picks and had to use black powder to blow up big chunks of frozen dirt. Bossman shook his head. "By cracky, when that snow and ice melts in the spring, they are going to have a mess."

One evening Sunshine was sitting on a crate, playing with her doll, while I finished scrubbing the rice pots. Suddenly, my father entered the cook tent. He was using a crutch and his foot was bandaged.

"A log crushed my foot," he said, without any greeting. "It will heal, but we are returning home."

"Honorable Father," Sunshine exclaimed, jumping off the crate and running to him. I had not told Sunshine that I had defied our father to bring her here. I wanted to spare her feelings.

My father ignored her and, turning his back on her, said to me with anger in his eyes, "You have disobeyed me! You have brought shame to me and your ancestors!"

I put down the rice pot and stood up to face him. I would not back down from him this time. "I am sorry, Father, but I think my ancestors would be happy that I did not leave one of their descendants in slavery," I said.

Sunshine stood there, mouth agape, shocked at the outburst. With tears welling in her eyes, she looked first at me, and then at our father. Father turned and limped to the door. Then he stopped. His voice shook violently with anger.

"I will tell your mother that she only has two sons now. You will never be welcomed back in the Celestial Kingdom." He walked out.

Sunshine cried, sobbing fitfully. "Our father has disowned you because of me."

I hugged her. "No, Sunshine. Our father is a stubborn man. He has not been happy with me for a long time. We will stay here and make ourselves a good life."

We watched from the cook tent as my father limped away. He did not look back.

In my mind, I had imagined my father having a change of heart when he saw Sunshine in person, although Zhang Wei had warned me that would not happen. I tried to remain cheerful for Sunshine, but there was an ache in my heart that would not be healed soon. Zhang Wei and Bossman were even more kind when they learned what had happened. Zhang Wei heard that my father was staying in Sacramento until his foot healed. I had a letter written to my mother, hoping it would arrive before my father returned home. I knew she would never defy my father, but perhaps she would take comfort knowing Sunshine was safe with me.

*****

The two railroads were supposed to connect, but both railroads just kept on building, trying to gain more money and land. The Union Pacific graders were making grade parallel to ours. Sometimes the lines were only a few feet apart. The Irish workers threw frozen chunks of dirt at the Chinese workers and shouted taunts and insults. When my countrymen continued to ignore them, they attacked them

with pick handles. To their surprise, my people fought back. Next, the Irish set off charges without warning and two men from another crew were hurt. A few days later, a huge explosion went off from our side. None of the Irish workers were seriously hurt, but they got the message, and there was no more fighting.

Much of this hard work was a waste because the tracks were finally set to meet at a place called Promontory. But before that happened, Mr. Crocker and Doc Durant, the head of the Union Pacific, made a bet. For weeks, the bosses had been pushing the men to lay track faster and faster.

The Union Pacific bragged that they had done four-and-a-half miles in a day. The Central Pacific did six. The Union Pacific set the tracklayers to work at three in the morning, using lanterns for light. Long after dark they announced they had done eight miles.

Mr. Crocker bragged that his men could do ten miles in one day.

"He bet Durant ten thousand dollars, but Strobridge doesn't think they can do it," Bossman told me. "But Mr. Crocker says he has it all planned out."

Mr. Crocker picked a good spot only a few miles from Promontory, Utah, where the railroads would finally meet.

April 28 was chosen as the day. The leader of the Union Pacific came with several of his engineers so he could laugh at Crocker and Strobridge when they failed.

Mr. Crocker had five supply trains ready by dawn's first light. Each train had sixteen cars loaded with enough material to build two miles of track. At dawn the Chinese workers jumped on the first train, unloading the materials. Then the train was backed onto a siding and the second train was ready to go as soon as the first two miles were finished. Each man knew his job, and Crocker arranged his plan so carefully that not a second was wasted. When the whistle blew for the meal break at one thirty in the afternoon, the workers had already laid six miles of track. We served the workers quickly so they could use part of their hour to rest, but they knew they had won. When the day was over, they had gone more than ten miles.

That Sunday, I sat with Bossman and Zhang Wei while they played their game of poker. Now that we were only a few miles from the end, I felt a deep sadness. Would I ever see Bossman or Zhang Wei again? They had been my friends for three years. And what was I going to do? How would I ever earn enough money to care for myself and Sunshine?

"They are building railroads all over," Bossman said. "Not as grand as this one, but they are going to need help."

"I don't want to have Sunshine grow up like this. She needs a home."

Sunshine took my hand. "Do not worry so, Elder Brother. I am happy to be wherever you are."

"I thought you were coming to live with us," Sam suddenly said from the doorway. "My mother is going to be very unhappy if you don't. She's already made a pretty room for Sunshine. You'll have to share a room with me."

I whirled around to see his wide grin. "I thought you weren't coming back," I said.

"Why would you think that?" Mr. McGee said, coming into the room after his son. "I thought we had a deal."

"When you didn't come back, I thought you had changed your mind because of Sunshine," I admitted.

Mr. McGee twirled his long mustache. "I'm sorry it took so long for me to get back. I had to make sure my wife liked the idea, and then we had to get the house ready for two new people."

Sunshine tugged at my coat. "What does this mean, Elder Brother? Are we going to live in Mr. McGee's house?"

Mr. McGee knelt down beside her. "Would you like that?" he asked gently.

Sunshine looked at me. "Will I be the servant?"

"No, silly," Sam spoke up. "Mama will make you do a few chores—we all do some. But you'll be like a Chinese cousin come to visit."

"I think that as a member of our household you will be protected from all the people who don't want any Chinese in this country. Surely, this hatred won't last very long.

After all, millions of people living in this country were immigrants from somewhere," Mr. McGee said.

Before we left for Mr. McGee's home, he had to stay and take pictures of the ceremony when the two railroads finally met.

"Do you realize that you have been part of one of the biggest building projects in history? Many people are calling the transcontinental railroad the eighth wonder of the world. Where the trip took six months by wagon, now a person can travel from coast to coast in about six days."

The Central Pacific was done at the end of April, but the Union Pacific was not. The ceremony was set for the eighth of May, and then postponed until the tenth. Most of camp was empty now. Men had either gone back to China with their savings or obtained other jobs on other railroads or farms. Zhang Wei had received notice that his new bride was waiting in Sacramento and that the agent had procured a small storefront suitable for a restaurant. My heart was heavy to see him go, but Mr. McGee said he would make sure we saw him, since we would be in the same city. Bossman stayed until the last day because there were still a few men left to feed. He had been offered a job at a small railroad in Oregon. He promised to write.

May 10, 1869, was cool and clear—one of those beautiful spring days. There was a crowd of six or seven hundred spectators. Promontory was not a scenic place.

It was five thousand feet high in altitude, but it was a flat valley about three miles across. Little grew there except for sagebrush and scrub bushes. The Union Pacific locomotive #119 was at the end of the track facing west. The Central Pacific's locomotive, the Jupiter, faced east. Between them lay a gap in the rails. At the signal, Chinese workers carried one rail and dropped it in place. Irish workers did the same on the other side.

"I can't see," Sunshine pouted.

Bossman swung her up on his giant shoulders. I smiled at how American she had become. In China, she would have never complained.

There were several other children, mostly the reporters' children and, of course, Strobridge's family, who had been with him the entire journey. Then Leland Stanford—Mr. McGee said he was the governor of California and one of the owners of the Central Pacific—and Doc Durant took a special silver hammer and tried to drive the spike in. They both missed and I heard several chuckles. Then Grenville Dodge, the construction manager for the Union Pacific, took a regular hammer and drove in the spike.

Everyone broke into cheers and clapped. I was so busy helping Mr. McGee with his picture that I had hardly noticed. If you are the photographer, you are always too busy taking pictures to take part in an event.

Sunshine hugged Bossman. I shook his hand the American way. "Jumping Jehoshaphat!" I said. "It has been good to know you."

Bossman grinned. "By cracky! I think Sunshine is learning English even faster than you, Chin."

I helped Mr. McGee pack the camera and developing tent. We were all taking one of the first trains back to Sacramento. It didn't seem possible that it was over. I said as much to Sam.

"It's not over," Sam said. "With the railroad, the country will really grow fast."

We climbed aboard the train heading west. I looked out the window as the train went full speed ahead on the track. All the towns that had been my life for the past three years flew past in a blur.

Sunshine looked out the window, too. "We are having an adventure, aren't we?"

I smiled and said, "Yes, we are having a wonderful adventure."

the end

The Real History Behind the Story

L ee Chin is a fictional character, but many of the events and incidents in the book are based on fact.

Building the Transcontinental Railroad

The idea of a transcontinental railroad had been talked about for many years, but it was dismissed as impossible. When gold was discovered in California, the idea was proposed again. Travelers to California had three choices. They could go in covered wagons, a trip that took six months. They could sail around the dangerous tip of South America, which also took about six months. And third, they could shorten the time by going across the Isthmus of Panama and risk dying of yellow fever.

The main obstacle of traveling by land was the high, snowy Sierra Nevada Mountains on the eastern border of California.

Finally, a man named Theodore Judah discovered a route using an old trail by Donner Lake. He interested several businessmen in his idea and they formed the Pacific Railroad company. Judah made many more trips to Washington, D.C., to get funding for the new railroad.

President Abraham Lincoln signed the Pacific Railroad Act in 1862, setting up two railroad companies, the Central Pacific and the Union Pacific. The two companies would build the railroad toward each other from the east and west. This map shows the route of the railroad.

The president, Abraham Lincoln, was interested, and he signed the Pacific Railroad Act in 1862. It set up two railroads, the Central Pacific in the west and the Union Pacific in the east. They would build toward each other until they met. In addition to financial assistance, each railroad would get 6,400 acres (later this was doubled) in addition to the land the railroad and its buildings were on. The Civil War delayed the start of the Union Pacific until 1865. The Central Pacific, led by

Chinese workers were an integral part of building the Central Pacific railroad. These Chinese men are seen working near what would become the first opening of the Summit Tunnel.

Charles Crocker and Leland Stanford, who would soon become governor of California, hired a capable construction supervisor named James Strobridge. But they had a lot of difficulty hiring enough workers.

Hiring Chinese Workers

James Strobridge was doubtful when Charles Crocker proposed hiring Chinese workers. The average Chinese man at that time was four foot, ten inches and weighed one hundred twenty pounds. When he hired a few as a trial, however, he discovered they were very steady, hard workers who out-worked the bigger, stronger Irish workers every time.

There were many Chinese living in California already, who were drawn to the United States by the discovery of gold in 1849. Many of them came from southern China, driven away by a period of famine caused by weather and a terrible civil war called the Taiping Rebellion. Eventually, even more would be hired by agents sent to China.

The Six Companies, each representing a particular province in China, also provided help to the Chinese workers. They arranged passage to America, handled the money sent back home, and took care of other problems for the men.

Women, however, were not highly valued in Chinese culture. In a largely agricultural society, sons were needed to help with farming. A girl belonged to her husband's family after marriage, but a son brought his wife home, thus providing grandchildren to care for the elders. Female children were often abandoned or sold into slavery, especially in times of famine

The first Chinese immigrants were, if not welcomed, at least tolerated. But as people crowded into California and the gold rush ended, resentment grew against the Chinese. The whites felt that the Chinese took away jobs and kept wages low. Later, immigrants were not

The Chinese workers faced harsh treatment and physical conflicts with white workers. This is an artist's drawing of a violent incident between Chinese and white rail workers.

treated well in America. They were not allowed to become citizens and were not allowed to testify in court. This meant they had no protection when they were beaten or robbed by whites. Many of these harsh laws were not repealed until just before World War II.

Working on the Railroad

The Chinese and the white railroad workers (mostly Irish) were paid about the same by the Central Pacific. But room and board was provided for the white workers and they were given the better jobs, such as foreman. The Chinese had to provide their own room and board. They divided themselves into groups of about thirty, each with a headman and a cook. Young boys like Lee Chin were often mess attendants and they carried tea to the workers.

Because the Chinese workers drank hot tea, which had been boiled, they got sick less often than the white workers, who drank from streams and rivers. The Chinese also ate a well-rounded diet of vegetables, fish, pork, chicken, dried mushrooms, and rice. The white workers ate beef, potatoes, and beans.

The Chinese workers bathed every day after work, to the amazement of the white workers, who seldom bathed.

The Chinese people said their family name first. For instance, if you were John Smith in the United States,

This is a famous photograph taken at Promontory Point after the completion of the transcontinental railroad on May 10, 1869.

in China, you would be Smith John. Boys were usually given strong names like Clever (Min) or Wise (Hue). Chin means "gold." Girls were usually given softer names like Sunshine.

Most of the white workers called all Chinese men John and the foremen were called China herders. Even though they were free men, the foremen sometimes beat or whipped their Chinese workers. The Chinese did try striking to combat this harsh treatment and to receive better wages. But when Strobridge cut off their supplies, they went back to work.

Mrs. Strobridge and her six children did live in a boxcar, which was divided into three rooms and followed the track. Strobridge's family remained with him the entire time, until the very last spike was driven into the railroad track at Promontory Point, Utah, on May 10, 1869.

Further Reading

Fiction

Mercati, Cynthia. *The Great Race: The Building of the Transcontinental Railroad*. Logan, Iowa: Perfection Learning, 2002.

Reichart, George. *A Bag of Lucky Rice: A Novel.* Boston: David R. Godine, 2002.

Yep, Laurence. *Dragon's Gate.* New York: HarperCollins, 1993.

Nonfiction

Halpern, Monica. *Railroad Fever: Building the Transcontinental Railroad, 1830–1870.* Washington, D.C.: National Geographic, 2004.

Olson, Nathan. *The Building of the Transcontinental Railroad*. Mankato, Minn.: Capstone Press, 2007.

Perl, Lila. *To the Golden Mountain: The Story of the Chinese Who Built the Transcontinental Railroad*. New York: Benchmark Books, 2003.

Renehan, Jr., Edward J. *The Transcontinental Railroad: The Gateway to the West.* New York: Chelsea House, 2007.

Uschan, Michael V. *The Transcontinental Railroad*. Milwaukee, Wis.: World Almanac Library, 2004.

Internet Addresses

Central Pacific Railroad Photographic History Museum
<http://www.cprr.org/>

Golden Spike National Historic Site
<http://www.nps.gov/gosp/index.htm>

Transcontinental Railroad—American Experience
<http://www.pbs.org/wgbh/amex/tcrr/>